Melanie Jackson Agency
250 West 57 St., Suite 1119
New York, New York 10107

W9-BRX-770

Lion at the Door

Lion
at the Door

A Novel by

DAVID ATTOE

LITTLE, BROWN AND COMPANY
Boston Toronto London

COPYRIGHT © 1989 BY DAVID ATTOE

ALL RIGHTS RESERVED. NO PART OF THIS BOOK MAY BE REPRODUCED
IN ANY FORM OR BY ANY ELECTRONIC OR MECHANICAL MEANS, INCLUDING
INFORMATION STORAGE AND RETRIEVAL SYSTEMS, WITHOUT PERMISSION IN
WRITING FROM THE PUBLISHER, EXCEPT BY A REVIEWER, WHO MAY QUOTE
BRIEF PASSAGES IN A REVIEW.

FIRST EDITION

The characters and events in this book are fictitious.
Any similarity to real persons, living or dead,
is coincidental and not intended by the author.

Library of Congress Cataloging-in-Publication Data

Attoe, David.
Lion at the door.

I. Title.
PR6051.T85L5   1989   823'.914   88-13954

10 9 8 7 6 5 4 3 2 1

Designed by Jacques Chazaud

FG

Published simultaneously in Canada
by Little, Brown & Company (Canada) Limited
PRINTED IN THE UNITED STATES OF AMERICA

For Linda, always

It's like a lion at the door;
And when the door begins to crack,
It's like a stick across your back;
And when your back begins to smart,
It's like a penknife in your heart;
And when your heart begins to bleed,
You're dead, and dead, and dead, indeed.

— Nursery rhyme

Hazel

"**I**'ve told you not to do that before."

I crawled under the table. I came out the other side and ran in the corner. I crouched down. The bottom of him vanished behind the table. His head and arms got bigger, coming after me. I shut my eyes. The black in there made me open them. It was all of him coming after me, bigger and bigger, going up in the sky. His boots stopped in front of my eyes. He came down and smashed my head. It hurt a lot to make me cry. He smashed it again and shouted very loud:

"You dirty little bugger. Told you not to do it, didn't I."

He went smaller. By the door he went small enough to fit. He went under it. I rubbed my eyes to see better if he came back.

I don't know how old I was.

We lived in a village with fields, and lanes with hedges with rodents and wild flowers in them, and a big round hill with bilberry bushes all over it, and skylarks' nests. Not far across the meadows with Friesians and sometimes Red Poll in them, and clover I looked for four leaves on, past the pond where the witch lived under the green slimy weed, over the stile and across Blackburn Road, was the pit the miners went down. Miners didn't have to go fight Hitler because the coal was more important. He was a miner, my father was. And my uncle Sid. I liked him better than my father. But Uncle Sid had bad lungs.

A lot of women my mother knew went to work in the pot factories in nearby towns. But my mother charred. She went to the big houses in the village to dust and scrub. She spent most time at Mrs. Marshall's. Mrs. Marshall was very bossy. She had a lot of silver things. It took my mother nearly one day a week just to clean Mrs. Marshall's silver. It made her hands all black doing it. Mrs. Marshall paid her a bit more an hour than others did so my mother had to stay with her. She had to look after my gran as well. My gran lived with us, downstairs in the front room, because she was old and could only get about with little steps and a walking stick. My brother Graham went to school. He was seven years older than me. He didn't like me much. Was always trying to get me in trouble. A sister would have been better.

"Come straight home," he said. "I don't want you messin' around after school. I've told you now."

He stood there, he was my father, with his hands in his pockets, very black and sooty from the pit, ready to have a go; the dust was clinging to his skin where his clothes stopped, gummed up by his sweat. Dust was soaked so deep and solid in his clothes that parts of the cloth looked spit and polished like the soldiers' boots when they came home in khaki, showing off their shiny black toe caps and clicking their heels as they walked about the village, all cocky. I was used to seeing him change color. It made no difference what color he was, black from the pit or white from the tub, he was always the same underneath. Uncle Sid was dead some time but it was funny because my dad kept saying he'd done Sid's shift for him. I asked Mum about it but she said she didn't know, he told her nowt, and as long as he fetched money home she didn't care what he did. Michael Zygadlo in my class said his dad knew my dad, that he didn't like him and because of some trouble at pit my dad had to give his dad some of his face work and my dad had to do some of his dad's surface work. Michael Zygadlo said he didn't know what the trouble was about, only what he told me.

"Yes, Dad," I said.

I left him in the house by himself. It was one of Mum's Marshall days and she'd gone early because there was no Granma to dress anymore (she died about when Uncle Sid did), and Graham was gone before Mum because his school was in town and he had to get the school bus opposite the post office at quarter to seven. I think him and Gerald Swindley got on first and bagged the back seat. I knew it went round the houses after that 'cause someone told me. My brother never told me anything. He was like that. Only time he had anything to do with me was when he wanted to make trouble.

I skipped to the end of the lane and I saw no one from the other houses. I scared the robin looking for food in the hollows and he flew into an oak and probably waited till I'd gone before dropping down again. And I sang to a made-up tune. . . . And when tomorrow comes it is today again when tomorrow comes it is today again. . . . The wind blew dust out of the hollows. . . . Everything now, summer and winter the same. Everything now. And yesterday. . . . Round the corner where the bus picks up Graham, I saw Mrs. Reade in the post office (I never ever saw Mr. Reade) through the window with the large clock in it that only had one hand. She was breaking up large sheets of stamps and when she'd torn a sheet into small squares she wrote in a big book. I skipped on by the church into the playground where I waited for Joan. We went in holding hands. Joan was my best friend in school.

Every morning we did reading and writing with Miss Carter (she called it English) and the others in my class struggled with it more than me and Joan, especially Valery Muchall, who had a stammer and couldn't get the words out for ages but Miss made her read anyway, and Vince Mott, who read all the *and*'s and *but*'s he could find on the page because he couldn't read any other words and Miss got mad with him. Joan was better than me at reading because she knew more big words (her mum was a teacher in another school). Spelling was harder. I wasn't much cop at spelling. Miss Carter was my favorite teacher by miles.

After break when the bell went we all ran in again bumping into one another and pushing, trying to get to our desks first. John Smodder was there already. He was always there, even before school started. He had something bad wrong with him so they wouldn't let him go play. Joan was first to finish the writing Miss set us, me second, and after I wrote my name on the paper I went over to Miss Carter's desk, where she was sitting watching the class and marking some books, and I jumped on her back.

"Don't do that, Hazel," Miss said.

And I did it again.

"I said don't do that."

And I did it again.

"That's enough now," she said. "I won't tell you again. I mean it."

I did it one more time clutching her as hard as I could. She became angry, tugging at me behind her back but I held on for quite a bit. I loved to jump on her and liked it more when she got angry and shouted. I ran out when the dinner bell went.

School dinners were horrible. They dished them out of those big cans. The metal made the spuds and the carrots taste funny. But the dinners were free so Mum said like it or lump it, and when it was sago pudding I lumped it 'cause it looked like frog spawn, and the one time I tried it it made me puke.

Mr. Blessed only came on Tuesdays. He took History and we got him first period after dinner. Mr. Blessed always had a dewdrop at the end of his nose. Most times he wiped them off with his jacket sleeve, sometimes his shirt; but they always came back quickly, like the drip on a tap. We played him up something rotten.

I looked round but Rosko wasn't at his desk. He never had school dinners.

"Put your books away," Mr. Blessed said. "Hand out the paper, John Bicker. One sheet each."

Mr. Blessed took the register and when he called Rosko's name Kenneth Brown said, "Here, sir." Kenneth Brown was the only boy in our class who wasn't afraid of Rosko.

"Number one," Mr. Blessed said. "How long ago did they start making pots, earthenware that is, and in which town?"

"You mean round here, sir?" Barry Preston said.

"That's the area we've been studying, isn't it," Mr. Blessed said. "Get on with it."

He had a tiny voice so most of the time he had to shout to be heard. When he was angry he squealed. Another dewdrop came on his nose. He wiped it and some of it fell on the floor. He saw and moved over it slowly and without looking down turned his foot on it.

"Number two, why did they start making pots in this area in the first place?" Mr. Blessed said. "Number three."

"Hang on, sir," Alan Fowles said. "I aren't ready."

"Number three, why were they called Butter Pot Towns?" Mr. Blessed said.

"Come again, sir," Brian Valant said.

"You heard," Mr. Blessed said. "Number four. Four and five go together. Number four, what was 'the hiring agreement'? Number five, what did 'good from oven' mean?"

"Very tasty," Kenneth Brown said.

He said it quiet but Mr. Blessed heard.

"I've had enough of you," Mr. Blessed said. "Every week it's the same. Come here."

"Me sir," Kenneth Brown said.

"Yes, you sir," Mr. Blessed said. "Now stand in that corner with your hands on your head."

"Hands on me head, sir?" Kenneth Brown said.

"Yes boy, hands on your head, if you can find it," Mr. Blessed said. "Face the wall. I'll deal with you later."

It was quiet for a minute while we were writing. Mr. Blessed cleared his throat and wiped off another dewdrop, trying all the time to keep an eye on Kenneth Brown as well as watch the class for cheating but he didn't see Barry Preston copy off Sheila Bishop in the next row and when he took his eyes off Kenneth Brown, Kenneth Brown made horns at him, wiggling his fingers.

Then the ones sitting along by the windows burst out laughing at something in the playground.

"Now what!" Mr. Blessed said.

"Nothing, sir," they said.

"Number six," Mr. Blessed said.

The laughing got louder and some of them in the next row stood up to look out and they started laughing. And soon all of us were over there to see. Mr. Blessed was frantic, dragging us one by one away from the window but as soon as he let go back we went. Then he saw for himself what it was.

"I'm not having this behavior in my class," Mr. Blessed said.

And he stormed out.

"Look at 'em," Joyce Bottomley said. "They's going round and round."

"T . . . tt . . . ttt . . . tt . . . thh," Valery Muchall said.

"How they get like that?" Colin Paltrey said.

"Not from kissing," Sheila Bishop said.

The two dogs were trying to go off in opposite ways,

pulling, and when the smaller dog pulled the big one yelped. Their bottoms were stuck together.

"What they doing?" Pauline Quinn said.

"I dunno," I said.

The big one yelped again when the small one gave a tug to get loose and the big one started to go backwards, the same direction the small one was going, like engines do sometimes, and then the small one tried to lie down and that made the big one howl out really loud and the small one turned and tried to bite the big one and snapped its jaws a few times and growled but it couldn't reach.

"Sit down immediately, all of you," Mr. Fisher said.

We all ran back as Mr. Fisher stood there scowling. Everybody was afraid of him. He was the headmaster.

"If Mr. Blessed tells me when I come back at the end of the lesson that there's been one further iota of trouble this class will be on detention for two weeks," Mr. Fisher said. "Thank you, Mr. Blessed."

"Thank you, sir," Mr. Blessed said. "Number six, what are 'twifflers' and 'muffins'?"

"Sir?" Derek Hancock said.

"What?" Mr. Blessed said. "I'm trying to do number seven."

"Nothing sir," Derek Hancock said.

"Number seven, what was 'potter's rot'?" Mr. Blessed said.

"Potter's what, sir?" Barbara Gitting said.

"Rot," Mr. Blessed said.

"R-o-t, sir?" Barbara Gitting said.

"Yes, r-o-t," Mr. Blessed said.

"Thank you, sir," Barbara Gitting said. "R-o-t, rot."

"Number eight, name the towns which compose the potteries," Mr. Blessed said.

"What's compose, sir?" Alan Fowles said.

"Make up," Mr. Blessed said.

"You don't want real names then, sir?" Pauline Quinn said.

"Of course I want the real names, stupid," Mr. Blessed said. "What six towns are called the potteries when they're grouped together, so to speak?"

"Six, sir?" Brian Valant said. "Thought it were five."

"Six, Valant, six," Mr. Blessed said. "Change papers quickly. It shouldn't take a month of Sundays. C'mon now. Whose test have you got, Barry?"

"Pauline Quinn's, sir," Barry Preston said.

"What's the first answer on it?" Mr. Blessed said.

"Off hers, sir?" Barry Preston said.

"Yes, boy, not off the floor," Mr. Blessed said.

"Says 1600, sir," Barry Preston said.

"Sixteen hundred is right," Mr. Blessed said. "One mark. And the town?"

"Me sir?" Barry Preston said.

"Yes, you sir," Mr. Blessed said.

"Boslem, sir," Barry Preston said.

"Burslem is right, one mark," Mr. Blessed said. "If they've written Boslem instead of Burslem, half a mark. The town is Burslem, not Boslem. What's number two, Diane Dart?"

"Because of coal fields and clay beds round here, sir," Diane Dart said.

"Two marks," Mr. Blessed said. "Number three, Joyce Bottomley."

"Nothing, sir," Joyce Bottomley said.

"Nothing?" Mr. Blessed said. "Whose paper is it?"

"Alan Fowles's, sir," Joyce Bottomley said. "He's written nothing."

"What did you say on yours, Joyce?" Mr. Blessed said.

"Because of an Act of Parliament by Charles II said butter pots had be a special size and weight," Joyce Bottomley said.

"Very good," Mr. Blessed said. "Good to see someone knows his history. Two marks if they have Act of Parliament and size and weight. Number four, Hazel Sapper, 'the hiring agreement'?"

"A workman had to stay with the master who hired him for one year, I said. If he didn't he could go prison. The master could fire workmen anytime he wanted."

"Two marks," Mr. Blessed said.

"My dad's in union, sir," Michael Zygadlo said. "They can't fire him that easy."

"Keep quiet, Zygadlo," Mr. Blessed said. "Neville Rouse, 'good from oven'?"

"Pots what come out of oven with no cracks in them, sir," Neville Rouse said.

"No," Mr. Blessed said. "What have you got, Hilary Shufflebottom?"

"If a pot come out of oven bad, boss blamed worker for it. Then he wouldn't pay him."

"Right, that was called the 'good from oven' system," Mr. Blessed said. "Two marks. Number six, John Bicker."

"Twifflers and muffins is what they called plates," John Bicker said.

"Yes, but they distinguished the sizes of the plates,"

Mr. Blessed said. "You need to mention size to get a mark. 'Potter's rot,' Cynthia Bourne?"

"Means lead poisoning from the glazing mixture, sir," Cynthia Bourne said.

"Right, one mark," Mr. Blessed said. "Number eight, the names of the towns, Joyce Bottomley?"

"You asked me before, sir," Joyce Bottomley said.

"Oh. Who's not done one?" Mr. Blessed said. "Jennifer Mitchell."

"Fenton, Stoke-on-Trent, Hanley, Burslem, and Tunstall, sir," Jennifer Mitchell said.

"That's only five," Mr. Blessed said. "Need all six for two marks. What's missing, Valery Muchall?"

"Lr . . . Lrr . . . Long, Long . . . Longton, sir," Valery Muchall said.

"Right," Mr. Blessed said. "Add them up and pass them back."

We all scrambled to get our papers.

"Out of fourteen," Mr. Blessed said. "Anyone get fourteen? No. Thirteen then?"

"Me, sir," Joan said.

"Very good," Mr. Blessed said. "Twelve? No. Eleven?"

"Me, sir," me and Glenys Howard said at the same time.

"Good," Mr. Blessed said. "Those over ten?"

A few hands went up.

"Not bad," Mr. Blessed said. "Anyone under seven?"

Alan Fowles, Vince Mott, and Barry Preston put their hands up.

"To be expected," Mr. Blessed said.

Mr. Fisher walked in as the bell went and bent down

and said something to Mr. Blessed and he said something back. Mr. Fisher warned us again then told us to leave quietly. He went out first and stood in the corridor watching.

"Them dogs is gone now, sir," Sheila Bishop said as she walked past Mr. Blessed.

Rosko was in the playground standing under the horse chestnut tree we got conkers from. He was gazing at his cupped hands. Rosko had no little finger on either hand but nobody teased him, not even Kenneth Brown. Nobody asked him about it neither, because he was strong and had a temper, but he was nice to me. They said others in his family had the same thing, no little fingers. Sometimes when he was writing in class I sneaked a look. It was counting them what made it strange: three fingers one thumb, three fingers one thumb; because his hands didn't look frightening, and there were no scars or dents like he'd had an accident.

"Gis a look," Barry Preston said.

He dared to grab at Rosko's hands.

"Sod off," Rosko said.

And he kicked Barry Preston on the shin, hard, and Barry Preston cried and ran off to tell but Rosko didn't care. He still had his hands cupped tight.

"What you got there?" Brian Valant said.

"Wouldner you like to know," Rosko said.

"Be like that, then," Brian Valant said.

He mumbled it and turned and walked off and kicked the broken branch with leaves on into the middle of the playground. Rosko stayed where he was, his hands cupped.

He never took his eyes off them. I peeked to see what it was. Everyone else kept a distance now. I couldn't see. Over in the far corner of the playground there was a lot of noise from a huddle that must have had a fight in it.

"What is it, Rosko?" I said.

"See fer yourself," he said.

He pushed his cupped hands towards me, stretching without moving his feet, and pulled his thumbs apart so that I could see it fluttering in there.

"It's a red admiral," I said.

"How d'you know?" Rosko said.

"From that book in school," I said. "There's pictures of all different butterflies in it."

"I know where there's lots more," Rosko said.

"Where?" I said.

"I can show you," Rosko said.

"Where?" I said.

"Not far," he said.

"Tell me," I said.

"Down Vale, near Clemence's Farm, by the old ruins," he said. "There's a bush they all go for. I can show you. That's where I were in History."

"All right," I said.

I'd only been to the old ruins once and there were no butterflies there then. We could hear the noise from the fight just as loud the other side of the playground wall. Soon a teacher would go and break it up. They never let them last very long.

"Why don't you let go on it?" I said. "It don't like it in there."

"Okay," he said.

He let it go. It had left a lot of colored powder on his hands from trying to get loose. It was purplish black with white spots near the tip of its front wings and bright orange bands across all of them. It fluttered backwards and forwards in front of us then suddenly flew high so all we could see was its shape in the bright sky because its colors had gone. White clouds hurried over in the friendly breeze and we hurried too, in and out of the patches of sunlight, and sometimes Rosko was in a bright patch with me and sometimes I had one on my own.

"How d'you tell a butterfly from a moth?" Rosko said.

"Butterflies come out in the day and moths at night," I said.

"How d'you know," Rosko said.

"You've never seen moths banging at windows in daytime, have you."

"What about colors?" he said. "Can you tell from that?"

"I dunno," I said. "Moths don't have colors. Not what I've seen. They're dull-looking. They don't need colors anyroad."

"Why?"

"What would they want with colors in the dark," I said.

"Maybe they have special eyes or summat," he said. "Dogs can hear sounds we can't hear."

"But if they don't have colors why would they have special eyes?" I said.

"It don't matter," Rosko said. "It's butterflies we's after. C'mon."

When Rosko saw Mr. Clemence's oldest boy driving

the tractor down the Vale towards us he pulled me onto the grass verge and we walked along it trying to avoid the nettle clumps but I got stung once and Rosko rubbed a dock leaf on it and it went away. We got back down as soon as the tractor and trailer went by and we had waved to the boy and he had waved at me and Rosko. Summer buzzed all round us.

"This way," Rosko said.

And already he had one foot wedged in the dry stone wall. He had the start on me so he was first over but I wasn't far behind. I wanted to show him I could climb too. And I did. We stood in the pasture. Cows were chewing cud, swishing their tails to fight off the flies but it was useless because they landed again before the swishing stopped, and at the other end the flies were going in and out of their eyes and they shook their heads lazily to try to get rid of them. I think they knew it was a waste of time.

A public footpath cut across the meadow and at each end of it there was a stile set in the wall; one got you onto the track up to Clemence's Farm (which had a right-of-way through it) and the other one let you out into the Vale. I think Rosko liked climbing walls better. We crossed the footpath near the middle of the field and made for the far corner. People who lived on the ridge used the path through the farm to get to the center of the village or the bus stop for town.

Rosko said cows never graze near their own muck even when the pats are old and shrunken circles. I asked him how he knew and he said because he'd seen grass grow through them and around them, and when the muck was nearly all disappeared the grass would still be new green and uneaten. He said he was a bit afraid of cows and that's why he was keeping a long way off. I said cows' eyes make things look very big to them so he didn't have to be afraid because he would look bigger than they were so they wouldn't go near him. It made no difference. He kept an eye on them all the way across the field, turning round every few steps so he could, and some of the cows that had started grazing again stopped to look back at him, and one of them mooed deep and loud, stretching its neck out and lifting its head up.

We climbed the wall; this time I made it over fast as Rosko. We skipped down the slope then Rosko ran up again and said "Watch this" and he came down rolling and said for me to try so I did and he did it again faster and said we could do it two at once and we came down roly-poly all hugged together laughing as we rolled over and over each other.

The ruin had one very tall wall. It was very thick with half a window left at the top. Going the other way another thick wall was joined to one end of it, but it wasn't so high. There were some low walls you could jump on, and over the other side on its own was a long wall we ran along. In the middle some big stones stuck out of the ground and one had a big crack I squeezed in. Rosko picked a buttercup and came to the big stone and held it under my chin.

"You like butter," he said.

"It looks bigger than before," I said.

"What?" he said.

"That wall there with half a round window," I said.

"It can't," he said. "It's fallin' down."

"Well, something's different," I said.

"You," he said. "You's getting cow's eyes. C'mon."

"No I aren't," I said.

"C'mon, I'll show you. Round other side," he said.

"What did this used to be?" I said.

"I dunno but it were very big once," he said. "Bigger than a church. We have to get over there."

"All right, I'm comin'," I said.

This field had no cattle in and there were no cowpats I could see, only thistles, tons of them.

"The bush they're after is back here," he said. "Watch out, wall is crumbling."

"I'm all right," I said. "Stop mithering me."

"Look," Rosko said, "look at 'em all."

"There's hundreds of 'em," I said.

"Lots of them admirals," he said.

"They're not all admirals," I said. "That one's a comma, and that one there on the end of the flower."

"Miss Carter's always going on about them, isn't she," he said.

"Very funny, Rosko," I said. "Look, a painted lady."

"Never heard of them," he said. "It's got more spots than the admiral."

"Look at that one up there, near the top, with orange patches on its wings," I said.

"Yeah," he said. "Rest of it's white."

"Yeah," I said. "There's another one now right by it."

He didn't care what they were called. The colors and fluttering excited him enough.

We watched them panic over the purplish flowers and

green-gray leaves; more kept arriving and became hectic straightaway. I waved my arms and went "Shoo" and I did it again more, but they took no notice they were so crazy for the bush. We watched and watched them. After a bit I thought I heard voices.

"Someone's coming," I said.

"Quick," Rosko said.

He grabbed my hand. We hurried to the corner and pushed between the wall and bush and kept still. My heart went fast. Two boys, one short, one tall, came over the wall and went to the bush. They watched the butterflies. Then one of them had a piss, squirting it in the air in a circle, and after he did an S with it until there was none left.

"Who are they?" I said.

"They're not from here," Rosko said.

"How did they know about the butterflies then?" I said.

"Maybe they didn't," Rosko said, making his voice even quieter.

"They went straight to the bush," I said.

He was disappointed someone else knew about the bush. We waited and never took our eyes off them. They were close. The short boy grabbed a white butterfly and clutching it in his fist he went to his friend with it. He lifted it out to show him and pulled one of its wings off. The tall one smiled. He pulled off another for him and he smiled again. So he took one more, tearing harder this time, which excited his friend. Then he let go of the butterfly and they laughed as it spiraled down flapping its dud wing, and before they crouched to watch it squirm they laughed some more. The butterfly jerked round and round lashing against the grass blades and then at the steel cap of the short one's boot until he dashed it at the air and it crashed down and beat faster and the wing began to break apart as it pounded the flattened grass where his sole was before and it panicked its body, flicked it again and back over the shattered wings, still thrashing to make flight to get back to the bush and the tall one bent over to pick it up and he knocked the butterfly belly and head with a twig away from the thread of a wing still attached and rolled the fragment between his fingers, then loosed it, and it fell slowly, from side to side, and lay useless beside its body, which they left on the ground to wriggle to death.

"Get us another one," the tall one said.

He fetched him an admiral this time.

"Let's both pull," the short one said.

"Ready. One. Two. Three."

They ripped off its wings and let it fall and the tall one stabbed through it many times with the pointed twig and they both sniggered at it, riven on the ground, and ran back together to the bush for another one.

"There's a big bugger," the tall one said.

He jumped after it and missed. Rosko was out of the bush and had him to the ground before he could jump up again and was punching him in the face and the short one started to kick Rosko all over, who didn't stop punching his friend and the other didn't stop kicking Rosko. I ran out and kicked the one who was kicking Rosko and he turned from kicking him and kicked me and punched me in the face and I kept kicking him back and Rosko scrambled up from the one on the ground, who was bleeding, and jumped the other one and pulled him down and I kicked him on his way and Rosko, who was bleeding too, hit him in the face again and again and the tall one got up and ran off but Rosko held on to the short one and shouted at him not to do it again and that he would really mash him if he ever came back and I punched him and his nose was bleeding now and mine too where he'd got me with that punch in the beginning and Rosko let go of him and he ran after his friend. Rosko dusted off his clothes. His shirt was stained with grass, which he rubbed some more with the flat of his hand but it made no difference. We took some of the soft leaves from the bush and wiped the blood off us.

"You all right?" Rosko said.

"Yeah," I said. "Are you?"

"I'm okay," he said. "You's a good fighter."

"You showed them," I said.

"Not really," Rosko said.

He was waiting for me, lurking behind the kitchen door. Mum was at the sink peeling potatoes as I came in. He slammed the door. I jumped. He pounced.

"Where the hell you been?" he said. "I told you come straight 'ome."

"What's time," I said.

Before I could say he'd slapped me across the face and my nose began to bleed again and I tried not to cry. I must have thought that would stop him doing it. But he shouted louder and sloshed me again and that made me do it, and my face stung. I grabbed for Mum but he pulled me back.

"You bastard," she said. "Leave off."

But he never took no notice of her. He only stopped when he wanted.

"The little bitch," he said. "I'll show her. Come here, you."

I pulled away from him and held Mum. He came at me and Mum pushed me aside and stood in his way, the potato peeler still in her hand. He just stopped in time, rocking back a little.

"NO. Lay off," she said. "You shit, leave her alone."

He struck her across the head and it dropped to her chest. She rubbed the place then lifted her head high and screamed at him:

"Go on, you bastard, do it again, show you're a man."

I was frightened. I didn't think he'd stop now. He came at her again but then backed off; his arms went slowly to his sides, but the rage was still in him. He turned to me and glared and I looked at the floor.

"Where you been, Hazel?" she said.

Her voice trembled. She didn't want more hitting. Then she said as if I never belonged to her:

"Your dad said you was to come home."

I started crying.

"Hazel?" she said.

"I went look at butterflies," I said.

"Whaaa," he shouted.

"Me and Rosko from my class went look at butterflies down by Clemence's," I said.

The words came out in bits because I was gulping and crying and trying to talk.

"Butterflies be buggered," he said. "Next time. . . . Who's this Rosko when he's at home?"

"A friend," I said.

"What sorta friend?"

"A friend, I told you," I said.

"Don't get fresh with me, young lady," he said.

He raised his fist again and I jumped back. Mum was standing in the same place, gripping the peeler.

"Dunner want you messing with him no more," he said. "You hear me."

I tasted the salt again.

"You hear?" he shouted.

"Yes," I said.

"If you come late again I'll knock stuffing out of you. Now git up them stairs."

"Linden!" she said.

"You keep out on it," he said. "I'll show her. Who in the hell does her think her is."

I climbed up two at a time and shut my door. It wouldn't keep him out, I knew, but I felt safer with it closed. It was a tiny room and it was getting smaller. There was only just enough room for the bed, the drawers, which wouldn't open far because they hit the bed, and the straight-backed chair with chipped yellow paint, squeezed between the bed and the wall next to my lumpy pillow. A worn-out mat covered the little piece of floor; the end with the remains of tassels lay flat and the other stuck up because it had been folded over and sewn like that. Sometimes I made it unfold mile after mile on marble floors in palaces out of books, and I walked along it wearing long dresses and diamonds in my hair, which sparkled in mirrors; sometimes I made it stretch into the desert and it stopped at a deep hole with a rook hanging over it cawing; sometimes I rolled it up big as a Ferris wheel and got inside it at the top of a hill and rolled away. But most of the time it was just an old mat. Over my bed was a picture of Jesus standing in the clouds in a white veil with his arms held out. My mother put it there. I think it was my grandmother's once. At Sunday school we learned about the tricks he did but I never liked him much because he never did nothing wrong and he never did any of the things I asked him like when I asked him to help me and Mum kill my dad.

I sat on the bed. The ceiling was all brown from the leaks, and the wallpaper was peeling off in lots of places. The little pink flowers looked silly because their leaves were too big for them. I heard my brother come in and I heard his muffled voice and then I heard Graham's muffled voice too but I couldn't tell what they were saying. Mum ate after he'd gone to work. She never ate with him unless it was Christmas or something when we all sat together but even then she'd gulp it down and busy herself taking and fetching. The sound of her clearing away their dishes made me feel hungry. I stared at the cracks in the ceiling and tried not to think about it. After a bit they stopped talking and the next thing I heard was him leaving for the pit. He always slammed the door after him. I don't know how long I was asleep when the tapping on my shoulder woke me. She'd brought me some stew. She said nothing but I could tell by the way she moved he'd told her not to feed me. He must have threatened her. He did it all the time. She put the food down softly, and the glass of milk too, on the floor in front of the chair, kissed me gently on the head and tiptoed away. She turned and said in a whisper:

"Don't worry, luv. I didn't mean to. . . . I love you."

She turned to leave again and whispered:

"Don't let them see."

She pulled the door to but didn't close it. If my brother found out she'd given me the food he'd tell him about it. Graham didn't care. He'd do anything to get him on his side, so he could get away with things he'd kill me for doing. He was always spying, Graham was.

"I know, Mum, I shan't," I said.

I'm not sure she heard because I whispered too. She was silent going down the stairs. She always let me keep the light on but when he was home at night he'd make me turn it off. If he caught me with it on he belted me. So when he was working days I never did my diary. Nobody knew about it, not even Mum. Some nights I put a lot in it.

He's horrible horrible horrible. Wish he was dead instead of uncle Sid. Anty Fay is no fun no more. She dont smile without uncle Sid. I jumped on her again today. I still like it. Keep getting my spelling wrong in school. I know miss Carter likes me. But she told me talk proper again. Dont mean she dont like me. Means she does silly. When I talk proper like miss Carter says to, he says why you talkin stuck up and he calls me a stuck up bitch. He's always like it. Horrible. Miss Carter always talks proper. She says 'properly'. She never says 'proper' and

she does not drop h's like I do she says all the time and
g's. Hope Rosko is okay. His mum will see his shirt and
find out he was in a scrap. He will get in trouble. He
never said about his dad. Dont know if he has one. Ask
him tomorrow. Maybe he wont tell. He kicked Barry Pres-
ton when he asked about the butterfly. Rosko hates Barry
Preston. He's a boy. In the dream I was little again and
he came from the pit. I watched him in the tub and I
cant get off the floor. Went to see the butterflies. They
were pretty. Did rolypoly with Rosko. He smelled of grass.
We beat them boys and Rosko said I was good at fighting.

He hit mum hard. He does it all the time. Likes hitting
us. She could have stuck the peeler in him. Wish she
would. Promise never to tell on her if she did.

Hope I see Rosko in the morning.

Along the sand road Mum said it was a mile to our
school; bit less if you cut across the church yard you're
not supposed to. The path through the wood was shorter
but I didn't go that way unless someone else was going
because it was spooky in there on my own.

One Monday morning the boy in charge of the crossing
at the T junction outside school stopped me and threatened to send me back over the road and make me do it
again. I said I had crossed right and he said I hadn't and
when I asked what was wrong he said I crossed over
crooked. I said I did too cross straight and he shouted I
did not and made me do it again.

On the Friday Mum said she would come with me
because she had to get silver polish for Mrs. Marshall.
We walked through the wood. She was quiet. There were
rooks in there all talking and cawing at once very loud
but that wasn't why. She was miserable. He finished days

Wednesday and was back on nights without a break. They must have been fighting before I got home from school. She was quiet then too and I said nothing because I didn't know what to.

I thought I could smell them, the birds, musty almost, like warmed milk, but I didn't know what rooks smelt like so it could have been something else I smelled.

The same boy was there and we crossed almost together, Mum just a bit in front of me. He said nothing. As we were passing him Mum turned and said he was to leave me alone and that I knew how to cross a road and why was he picking on me. He went red. Her voice was hard like it could be when she was after something she knew she might have to fight for.

Joan said he never picked on her when I told her about him doing it to me. I remembered about Rosko's dad and asked her because she lived in the same road as Rosko. She said there was a man lived at Rosko's most of the time but he wasn't Rosko's dad and she knew because the man worked one of the cages at the colliery and her dad knew him and she'd heard her dad talk to her mum about him, about how he wasn't married to Rosko's mum, he had a wife somewhere else with three kids and he went back every now and then to see them but never stayed long.

The next week he was there again on crossing duty and he pulled a face at me as I walked by him but he said nothing. I never saw him taking it out on no one else and I thought maybe he went for me because I came to school on my own and I thought had I done something against him he was getting me back for. I worried about it for a long time and was glad when they replaced him with another boy and I didn't have to walk by him anymore.

It was windy and dull when I came out of school the first day the new boy was doing the crossing duty. I hurried across and I hurried along home.

"Now she's coming to sand road. Now she's turning into it. Now she's hopping to miss the holes that the robins and sparrows scavenge in. Now she's putting one foot in a hole and now she hops out onto the other one and then into another hole, bigger one, on the other foot and out again. Now she's coming to the turn onto the path which leads to the house up the little hill. She's wearing blue shoes with a strap over and white socks rolled down to her ankles because she doesn't like them up. She has a red dress on and it's got little white flowers on it and a stiff white collar. She doesn't like it much. It's too small for her now. Going home. Going home. She's slowing. He's not there now. Stop. She's stopped. Jump. She's jumping. She's hopping now. There's no holes in this part. One foot. Two foot. Up and hop and up and hop. She can do it in fifty to the top and touch the house in fifty. She starts from the telegraph pole with the white five painted on. Ready. Steady. Go. One two three four five six seven eight nine ten eleven twelve thirteen fourteen fifteen sixteen seventeen eighteen nineteen twenty twenty-one twenty-two twenty-three twenty-four twenty-five twenty-six twenty-seven twenty-eight twenty-nine thirty thirty-one thirty-two thirty-three thirty-four thirty-five thirty-six thirty-seven thirty-eight thirty-nine forty forty-one forty-two forty-three forty-four forty-five forty-six forty-seven forty-eight forty-nine fifty. Phew. Told you. Was fifty last time. It's always fifty. She's going round the back now to look at the rabbit. Her brother doesn't like her to touch it but he's not home. He won't know. You're a black and white Dutch, aren't you. He's called Freddy but she calls him Hopper. Hello, Hopper. She's putting her hand in to stroke Hopper. Nice Hopper. Here's some dandelion from the bucket. Look at your nose move. She's stroking his soft ears. She's closing the hutch door now. She's making sure so they won't know."

"Psst."

I jumped. Turned round. No one there.

"Psst. Over here."

I turned again to where I thought it came from.

"It's me, Rosko."

A branch of the bush with the little yellow flowers shook. He'd caught me talking to myself.

"You sod, Rosko," I said.

"Just teasing," he said. "I followed you all the way. You didn't know I were there. I like being invisible. Didn't mean scare you."

He came out of the bush. Yellow petals stuck to his jacket and some were in his shiny brown hair. He looked in the hutch and poked his finger through one of the holes in the wire mesh to stroke the rabbit but it flicked back fast and he couldn't. A little finger would have gone through far enough to reach but this was the wire they use down the farm with tiny holes, two layers thick, on the ferret cages.

"If you was just trying hide why'd you make me jump?"

"I want show you somethin'."

"You didn't have make me jump fer that."

"Nobody else knows."

"Yeah, why you telling me?"

"I like you."

"What is it?"

"You'll see when we get there."

"Where?"

"Dingle. It's in dingle."

"What?"

"You'll see fer yourself. You comin'?"

"My dad'll give me what for if —"

"We'll get back before he comes home."

I knew about the dingle but I'd never been there. The sides were very steep and people said there were adders crawling about down there and they said there were bear traps too from long ago, never sprung, and that if the snakes didn't get you first the snares would. When I told Rosko he said he'd heard that too but he promised there were no traps, not anymore, and many times he'd seen snakes in there but only grass snakes and they weren't poisonous. I think it seemed to take a long time to get where we were supposed to be going because Rosko said nothing as we went. He concentrated as he walked, and he seemed to listen to the wind, as if it told him where to go, whispered to him what lay ahead. I knew it wasn't really true but Rosko had such a funny way with him. Maybe he was just playing at being invisible.

The sky was very heavy but Rosko continued at the same pace and not knowing where we were I had to stick with him. I wanted to anyway. I knew that trying to get him to hurry for shelter was useless; this was Rosko's secret and he would let go of it when he was ready; the threat of rain would make no difference. Rosko did things always the same, stubborn, like he knew only one way, as if he had to be like that to be Rosko, as if he believed he wouldn't be Rosko anymore if he wasn't like that. I liked him the way he was, and so did he. The other kids in school kept away from him. But I think he was on his own a lot because he wanted to be, not because they left him alone. He knew I liked him and now he'd said he liked me I could really be his friend.

We got to the top of the dingle, which was fenced off from the field we'd just crossed to stop cattle wandering in there and falling or getting stranded, but I kept thinking, because of what I was told, it was there to stop nasty things getting out but I never said that to Rosko. I wanted to talk, make enough noise, shout even, to try to scare away any beastie in there hiding. We were going in. Whatever was in there I wished like mad it wasn't.

The fence stretched as far as I could see both ways. I watched Rosko, waited, and kept quiet. He was going in. The sky rumbled and bumped and spilt a few drops of rain on us. Rosko opened the fence. It opened like a gate off one of its hinges would. The wires were cut but when the fence was in the proper place you couldn't tell there was anything wrong with it.

It was very dark now all across the field and further and the sky was picking up speed as it raced over us, spinning and leaping and overtaking itself. Any second it would bucket it down. In there it was even darker. I stared at the black, trying to make things out. Rosko put the fence back in place and stamped the earth down round the post, and instead of having that safe feeling when a door is closed by someone you trust, I was frightened; from this side the fence was more threatening, its little silvery barbs waiting to pierce, wanting to hurt now.

We went down a slanted path, one Rosko knew well he went so fast. He said it was the best way to go because going straight down from the top was dangerous, I'd see. He was way ahead of me. I said "I bet you can do this with your eyes closed" and he laughed. I stopped and turned and looked back and I couldn't see the barbed wire anymore. Now there was the dark. I tried not to be afraid but I'd come with fears. Rosko turned because he couldn't hear me following. I could only just make him out. He came back to where I was and grabbed me, gently, and we stood, me trembling and him holding me round my arms while the rain pelted the treetops up there and the leaves made an umbrella for now, and Rosko said he knew it here and that the things they said were lies, it was safe, he'd been here on his own lots of times and at first it scared him, but he wanted to like it because it was secret, and his tears soon went, so he told me not to be afraid.

High above us some lightning got through. Thunder clapped loud. It was very close, I counted. The dingle shook and drops of rain, small ones, began to hit us, but soon they were big because the rain was too heavy for the leaves to keep out. We went down deeper and Rosko stayed nearer to me but he had to shout for me to hear. Water was running over our faces.

"Be careful," he said. "Not far now."

The ground began to give way. It slowed us. We tried each step to see if it was safe. It was still a long way down to fall. Rosko stopped and shouted with his hands cupped over his mouth:

"Smell that?"

"It's horrible, what is it?"

There was an old tree trunk all decayed but it wasn't that and he pulled some creeper back from the trunk, which seemed to be feeding off it, and pointed down to the ground under it to this sticklike fungus, ugly, and smelling, smelling rotten.

"Dunno, found it yesterday. Bet you wouldn't eat it."

The rain drummed down. He was smiling.

"You eat it, if you like it so much," I said.

He let go of the creeper branch and it sprung back and covered the thing but the smell came off just as bad and further down I could still smell it, and after I couldn't I imagined I was, and then it wouldn't go away, and I thought it was coming from me, the smell. The rain suddenly heaved sideways across the dingle, lashing our faces, and we went together holding hands, sliding in the mud a lot.

Rosko shouted we were there but all I could make out through the spray was a big rock sticking out of the side of the dingle. It looked like it could fall any minute. I shut my eyes. I opened them again. It was still there.

Rosko went first and when he got up he said for me to follow. I jumped, gripped on the rope, and held tight, hanging like the pendulum on Mrs. Marshall's grandfather clock Mum showed me once when she took me cleaning when Mrs. Marshall was away. My feet fumbled for the footholds. There was a smell of fresh leaves and under it the smell of the drenched earth.

"Bit to your right," Rosko said. "Steady. Up a bit. There. Stop. Hold it. Put your foot in now."

He was leaning way over the top. Now the left foot was holding, he helped guide the other one in and after that he let me do it by myself. I watched my hands slide up the rope and grip again, and brown water from the rope ran over my fingers and down my arms. The rope moved, and me with it, as I felt for the holes he'd chipped in the rock. It got easier to climb and I was soon near the top. Rosko held down his arm and I grabbed it and he pulled me the last bit and while he was pulling I felt light as a feather. I ran on with the force of his pull and before I stopped he shouted:

"That's it. That's it over there."

I looked up, saw sheer crumbly rock above us all the way up with some trees sticking out of it.

"Not up there," he said.

He pointed with both arms at once to get me to it faster.

"There? That's it?"

His arms were fixed, pointing. There was loam and leaves and creeper and moss piled on the rock, leaning against the side of the dell in a big heap. That's what he was pointing to.

"What is it?"

We were both pointing now.

"My hut. My hut's the secret."

I went over to it.

"You wouldn't know it was there, would you," he said.

He pulled a square clod from the side of the heap and put it down. The rock we were standing on was very flat and smooth. He fiddled where the clod had come from until he opened a small door. Chicken wire held the leaves and creeper to the door. Rosko ducked and went in. I bent down to look.

"You'd never know," he said.

He lit an oil lamp and held it over by his grate; it was a cast iron one with a place for a kettle and teapot, which he had, one sitting each side, and it had a small oven. He struck another match against the metal to light the fire laying there ready: newspaper scrunched up under a pile of twigs, that looked like a crow's nest, with some small bits of coal on top and two logs. It was still dry.

"Come in. Put wood in hole. You can sit there. It's warmest place when the fire's going."

The paper flared up one piece after another and was gone but it caught the twigs, which began to snap and spit. Rosko turned round with his lamp and looked behind me. He had a table and two chairs, all with their legs sawn short. He put the lamp on the table. You had to stoop to move round because the roof was very low. The springs were gone in my chair so I sank down a long way; I must have been almost touching the floor. Rosko stayed stooping. He moved like that as if he'd always done it.

"I scavenge for coal on the slag heaps," he said. "Sometimes I get a big bit."

He tapped the top of his grate. It had flowers stamped into the metal in an arch at the top.

"Had a hell of a time getting that bugger down here."

"Where'd you get it?"

"Found it in the abandoned farmhouse at top of dingle. It'd been prized outta kitchen wall, just lying there. It were perfect for what I wanted. Lead were gone from roof so I figured who were after lead meant for grate and all, for scrap. Anyroad, they never took it. Get a better price for lead. They left none of that. Had a struggle with it. It were a sod. Dropped it a few times, I'm tellin' you, trying to get it in barrow. In the end I weighted barrow down, got one side of grate leaning against it, then levered other side up, bit at a time, holdin' it with blocks till it were level so I could slide it in. Wheeled it after to top of dingle and left it there in barrow under some tarpaulin I found."

He got two logs from the oven where he put them to dry out and tossed them on the fire and put two more from a pile near the door in the oven. It was getting warmer now.

"Went back next day after school. It were still there. Pushed it down field and got it up there right above hut."

He tried to show where he meant but his arm hit the roof.

"Tipped it just inside fence then covered it with leaves and branches. Rope I used on barrow were no good for lowering it down on. Took nearly a week to find summat decent. Looked all over. Nothing in farm sheds when I fetched barrow back. Nothin' in school caretaker's yard so I went down where Scabby keeps his lorries. He had dogs in there. Big scrawny buggers ready to tear your arse out. So that were that. Bet he had one and all. Then one time I were walkin' back across fields I remembered. There were one on scaffolding at Fratton church when

I went looking for barn owls' nests. It were still there the night I went back. I climbed up about level with clock, clock had sacking over its hands and face. I pulled the rope off builder's wheel. Then like a fool let go on it. It went crashing down making a hell of a noise against the poles. I lied flat in case someone heard and came looking."

Rosko sat down in the other soft chair and rubbed at his knees. We gazed into the fire. I thought, This is what old people do only they don't say anything. Rosko was fixed on the flames.

"What happened then?"

"Oh, I got away with the rope that night, hid it bottom of our garden. Foreman must have cursed some man next morning for not pulling rope up before he knocked off."

He laughed, and rubbed at his knees again, leaned forward, and cupped his hands round them. The lamp flickered when some wind got in.

"Couldn't do anything for a couple a days. Had to help me mum after school. With that rock up there I had be careful. Cast iron cracks easy. Tied one end of rope to grate and other end to a tree, leaving some over on grate end after the knot. Only way I could get a grip was to sit with my legs round the bottom of the tree. Got it started with my feet then pulled hard as I could on rope to slow it up. Had some old gloves but it still burnt a bit. I could never have held it back on my own. When all the rope was used up I let grate hang there, climbed down to where it was and secured it with the leftover rope to another tree. Then I climbed back up and untied the other end, then down again with it. I went like that from tree to tree till it reached here. Were a right game. Grate went so fast one time there was this loud creaking. Thought I'd had my chips, but the tree held. Were dark by time I got done."

He stopped talking but I think he went on with it in his head, went over how he got the grate in place, got it through the roof, fixed the chimney so it wouldn't blow smoke back in, so it wouldn't let water down, rebuilt the roof, and got the Zeebrite without his mum knowing so he could polish the grate until the black shone. I don't know if he knew he wasn't talking. His lips went on moving like he was.

Outside it was still raging. The gaps between the thuds made by the rain hitting the roof got shorter and shorter until I couldn't hear one from another, only a long boom added to the fury out there.

"Does it leak?"

"Hasn't yet. There's corrugated iron two thick under the turf and stuff. Ought keep it out."

It was hard to take your eyes off the fire. Rosko moved his chair a bit nearer. Then he stood up as straight as he could and began to unbutton his shirt as he shook off his shoes.

"What you doin'?" I said.

"Gotta get out these, I'm catching me death, I can't get warm. You're shiverin' too."

"But —"

"I won't look. Anyroad I know what's under there."

He reached under the table. There was a big Kellogg's box there. He pulled out an army blanket and threw it to me.

"I've seen. Animals 'ave same things, don't they. I've looked at them enough times. Bulls' balls nearly touch ground."

He didn't look at me when he said it; he was turned at the fire again. I grabbed the blanket, took my clothes off fast as I could, and huddled it tight against me. I felt afraid, and excited. . . . *Not no no . . . It was . . . No. . . . It's different*, I thought. . . . I felt my face flush and my stomach got butterflies. When I looked up he had a blanket round him too. He got another one out of the box and wrapped it round me to try to stop me shivering. His teeth started to chatter. We went nearer the fire and he put more logs on and blew on it to get it going faster.

We stopped shivering only when the fire was blazing. Our clothes began to steam on the line we'd made by fixing Rosko's S-belt above the fireplace to nails, which were hammered into the wood before he found it. When the kettle boiled we warmed the teapot and warmed our hands more on it, taking turns to hold it and swish the water round in it, and Rosko joked about not forgetting one-for-the-pot, and we made the tea and drank it weak from his chipped enamel mugs and I began to count the chips on mine but gave up soon past twenty because I didn't know which ones I'd done and which I hadn't.

More thunder came and some bits of soil fell on the table and Rosko got some in his mug. We both looked up and down just as quickly because it started again and we got some in our eyes. I thought the roof was coming in it shook so bad. Rosko looked at me.

"I built it strong, it'll hold."

He chucked the dregs from his mug on the fire. It hissed at him. He topped my mug up and filled his own too full but he got it on the table without spilling any. He ripped a piece of cardboard from the flap of the Kellogg's box and tore it in two and put one over his mug and gave the other piece to me for mine.

"She don't like you doing that jumpin'."

He surprised me saying that.

"But I do."

The fire trembled, fell on itself, and coughed. I hoped, but I knew he wouldn't let it go yet. Angry sparks jumped out and disappeared before they reached us.

"She don't," he said.

I wanted to tell him yes.

"Why d'you keep doin' it?"

No no, I thought. . . . He knows. . . . It's not only me if he knows. . . . Does he want to take her off me. . . . He's a boy. . . . She only wants me, doesn't she. . . . I'm her favorite. . . . What's he saying it for. . . . She likes me best.

"What's matter, Hazel? Why you cryin'?"

He came over and held me and said it was all right and I knew then he couldn't know why I was, and I wasn't going to tell him if he asked, but he didn't, just held me some more. I soon stopped crying. Rosko stayed in the chair with me and we talked about school and kids we knew and about how he'd never seen the sea and how he wanted to one day 'cause it must be a magic place, and about when he was older he wouldn't mind living in a hut but he'd build the roof higher so he could stand up. He said if he had a hut he could keep away from other people because most of the time he liked it best on his own. I told him I liked flowers best. I wanted to be near them.

I saw Rosko curled up on the mat in front of his fireplace when I woke up. The hut was still warm but the fire was burned out, gray, quiet. I smelled it was morning first. The rain was stopped and there was some light coming under the door and the point of the triangle it made up didn't quite stretch to Rosko's head. I could not remember falling asleep. I was scared what he would do to me when I got home.

"Rosko."

I disturbed him but he stayed asleep.

"ROSKO."

He rolled over with his eyes closed.

"What?"

"It's mornin'."

"Bloody hell."

He jumped up, naked.

I'd never seen them before, boys' things, sticking out and pointed with the little pouch hanging underneath. . . . *I never opened my eyes when . . . the razor cold . . .* When he turned and grabbed his pants off the line his calves tightened and his buttocks were firm and smooth, and round like they'd come out of a jelly mold.

"My dad'll kill me," I said.

He took his belt off the nails and scraped himself doing

it and when he tried to thread it through the loops in his trousers it got twisted and I helped him. We were both frightened.

"We never went 'ome," I said. "What we going do?"

"Tell 'em we got stuck. We'll go together."

"Won't make no diff'rence what we tell."

"Tell 'em we was playing and storm come so we shelter'd in old farm and fell —"

He stopped and looked at me hard, his dark brown eyes desperate because he couldn't believe in his own lie, knew it wouldn't work.

"Don't know what else tell 'em that's any good," he said.

"Won't make no diff'rence what we tell."

"Why d'you keep saying that. Must be something."

He knew there wasn't. He struggled into his shirt and I looked up at him from tying my laces. We were caught already. He looked back at the ashes, then at me, then snatched a blanket off the floor and threw it but it missed the box. He left it where it fell.

"I know it's no good," he said. "But you won't tell on the hut, will you?"

"Never."

He opened the door, took a step back and reached round it for the tin on the shelf. He took something out and put it in his pocket. I couldn't make out what it was but the light flashed off it. He put the tin back; it had a picture of a little boy on it dressed in old-fashioned clothes sitting with a rabbit on his knee. When he turned round his hand was still in his pocket with whatever it was, turning it.

"Thanks for not tellin'. We can come again if they don't find out."

Steam was lifting off a patch outside the hut where a shaft of direct sunlight dazzled on the rock like a search-light.

"Will your mum hit you?" I said.

"No, the fella she sleeps with will."

"We have to go back, don't we. We could . . ."

I tried to make it go away by saying it but it wouldn't go. Rosko said nothing, just locked up his hut and fetched branches to lean against the door and some to throw on the top. He wanted to keep it secret whatever happened. We carried the big branch he pulled down from a dead tree together and laid it up against the side.

I knew with Rosko it was the man going to belt him hard now he'd got his excuse. Rosko knew with me it was my father going to strike me. He never needed excuses.

"*Gglurrlth gglurrlth.*"

" 'ello, William. Didn't see your mother downstairs when I come in. Am I late. You knew I'd come, didn't you. C'mon, let's get you done. Put you in chair. Change bed first, wash after. You can 'ave red trousers today. I washed and ironed 'em. After you can look through window. I'll bang up your pillows. Then you can look at trees move. You can wear the blue shirt with squares. Red and blue go 'gether. Up we come. There, that's good."

"*Gglurrlth.*"

"What you lookin' at? You lookin' at me, aren't you.

Yeah, it's a black eye. Never tripped and poked broom handle in it like I told Mrs. Ellow this mornin' when her stopped me coming out of Emerton's shop and said, 'My my, you's got a right shiner there. How'd you get that?' No, I never fell. That bastard Linden give it me. He's broke our Hazel's arm and all. When he fetched her to doctor he said she fell. Bloody liar. It's in plaster now after hospital X-rayed it. Broke in more than one place, they said. They know it weren't from falling, I'm sure. But if I tell on him they'll come and fetch her away and he'd kill me fer tellin'. He's hit her before. But never broke no bones. Where's it going stop. I want to tell on him but I don't want lose her. Nearly did tell once. Got as far as the Social Services in town, took the bus when 'e were asleep off nights an' told Mrs. Marshall I had go doctor for me knee but I just couldn't make meself go into office I were s'posed to go in, and when the man in uniform asked me, I said I were after National Insurance and 'e said I were in wrong place. . . . So I did me best cover it up what he done to her. Lied. Protected him. That's what I've always done, ain't it. Why don't they take him away. The lousy rat's no good to no one and he pisses up most of money he's meant bring home. They take your littleuns into care and leave pigs like him alone. Me and Hazel could go, leave the bastard, I thought of that. But where. I can't keep her and Graham and me. Graham might want stay, I dunno. If I went cleaning full-time it wouldn't be enough. Besides now I come here three mornin's, full-time wouldn't be much more than I'm gettin' already. Doctors'll know it weren't no fall from that picture they took. They're s'posed to tell if they. . . .

It says so in paper when they show what's bin done to them kids, cigarette burns, br —. . . . They told on Vera Tibbetts's little boy when his shirt got ripped in a fight in school and teacher saw burn marks on his arms. They came, and fetched him away screaming. Nothing 'appened to that fat slob of a father on his Alf, nothing. Vera said after she would go on the game than stay with him but she never went. I thought of it after. Going on the game. If I can do it with Linden Sapper, I can do it with anyone. Mind you I never go near him if I can avoid it. But who'd want me now. Look at me. Well past it. They wouldn't give me the twice over. Broke her arm. It weren't her fault, she's still a kid. Time's a bit different for kids, they ain't learned it right yet. But what does he care. Never lets up. Worse when he's had a drink. He weren't like it when I first went with him lest I were blind. When it started right after we were married I thought maybe 'cause he were in dark so much made him like it. But they's been going down and up in dark, miners have, since way back and they's not all like him. Went down pit from school, some never had school. My dad and his dad before him went down and his before him and his dad and all. Were him, I think, my grandad's father, what went down mine in a bucket; they went one at a time then, and were pulled up by a donkey on a rope. They weren't bad men from what my mother said. My father never beat none of us kids; he was kind till the day dust got him, God rest his soul. You know in winter miners scarce see daylight, and after snowdrops come, sometimes before crocuses am out, when he were able my father went in the lanes and fields, over Marshes Hill, likc they were his prize fer being in dark so long. He'd come back every time with same amazement for what he'd come by, a flower, or a hare skip by him so quick it were gone before he got a good look on it, or a bird flying over to some northern nesting place, or one singing in a hedge, or just a smell in the air. He'd fetch my mother mushrooms when he found any but he never picked the wild flowers, said they never belonged in vases. When I think. . . . How did I get that bastard of mine. . . . He fisted her, I couldn't stop him. Ran at him, beat against him, that's when he give me this. I fell and he kicked me as he were belting her. They'll take her away this time, I know. It can't be hid. P'raps it's best fer her. And my dad said get a good man there's nothing wrong in marrying a miner. He wouldn't let me take her doctor, said he didn't trust me. I told him she hadn't eaten anything and she said she had some 'bread and cheese' off a hawthorn bush with Rosko. That did it. 'I'll give you Rosko,' he said and he slapped her, shouting, 'If I hear his fuckin' name again. . . .' Oh I'm sorry. I forgot myself. This zip's broken. Might be able fix it. If I can get this tooth loose. There. Let's pull you forward so I can do your pillows better. Now you can look at the trees move."

"Gglurrlth."

After the plaster was put on I stayed away from school for two weeks. The doctor told me I mustn't write with my right hand until she'd taken another X ray. I liked hcr. She gave me a pen with a light in it. He didn't like her. The day he dragged me to the doctor's he said he

wanted to see the man doctor but the woman in the ny-
lon overall told him we had to see who was taking surgery
or see no one. He said at first we'd come back another
time but the woman said that that arm looked like it
needed seeing to pretty bad. He stared at her but she
never flinched. He grabbed me and we sat down. The
other people waiting pretended not to notice us. When
it was our turn to go in he poked me in the ribs and said,
under his breath, to make bloody sure I said what he'd
told me to.

Rosko wasn't there when I went back. Joan said he'd
not been to school for a week and she'd not seen him in
their street. She'd heard from another girl that he was
sick.

I made a real mess of writing with my left hand. My
name came out *Hazel Sawyer* It was real spider
writing. I was worried I would get behind because I couldn't
do the writing and Miss Carter wouldn't like me. But I
was happy when she said for me to stay behind two after-
noons after school was out and to bring my work to the
teacher's room. She gave me help in writing. We did
new words and spelling and practiced sentence building.
She said again it was because I didn't talk properly made
the writing come out wrong. She gave me some books
to take home saying that reading was a good way to learn
to write. I wasn't sure what she meant but I read them
anyway. They were good stories.

I sneaked the books into the house because he'd have
taken them off me if he saw them. He said books were

bad and he wasn't going to have me getting evil in my
head.

Just after I got the cast I was coming down the stairs
trying to do up the buttons on my blouse with one hand
when Mum came in from doing the spastic boy. I stayed
in my room if Mum was out and he was down there, off
his shift.

"Let me help you."

"Thanks, Mum, it's hard with one hand."

"It's hard with two when your fingers am cold."

"How long does it have stay on?"

"Another three weeks fer definite were what hospital
said."

"It's heavy."

"I know, don't get swinging it about."

She hung up her coat and filled the kettle. She looked
tired and pale.

"You okay, Mum?"

"Me. I'm all right. Does you arm 'urt?"

"Aches a bit but not like when he done it."

"Why don't you sit with me while I do the spuds."

I managed to get onto the edge of the table and I sat
dangling my legs. The kettle boiled. She made some tea
and said did I want a biscuit with mine and I said yes.
They had sugar on them, and we dunked them in our
mugs and pieces fell off, and floated on the top, because
they were too soggy to get in your mouth without breaking.

"Mum?"

"What?"

"D'you know what 'appened to Rosko? He said he'd get in trouble and he hasn't been round or anything."

She finished her tea, tipping the mug right back, then rinsed it out and wiped her hands down her apron.

"Hazel, I want you promise me summat."

"What, Mum?"

"You won't have nothing more to do with Rosko."

"But Mum."

"I dunner want you going with him and you mustn't talk about him round your dad."

"Why?"

She never answered. She turned to the peeling. My stomach was tight and my throat went dry.

"Mum, he's my friend."

She put the peeler down, wiped her hands down her apron again, and came over to the table. I stopped swinging my legs.

"D'you know what 'appened to Mickey Tibbetts? Vera Tibbetts's little boy."

"What?"

"They took him away."

"Who did?"

"Them from Welfare."

"Where?"

"Put him in a home."

"What for, he's got one?"

"Special home where he'll get looked after and not get beaten all the time."

"Oh."

"If they find out about him hitting you. If he does it —"

She hugged me. I felt the tears against my cheek and I put my good arm round her and squeezed and I felt safe and scared together. She let go and kissed me and she went down slowly to the chair, her eyes cloudy, gazing.

"If he finds out you seen Rosko he might."

"I know, Mum. Promise I shan't."

A tear rolled down by her mouth and she wiped it off with the end of her apron. She tried to smile at me but it came out wrong. Her mouth twisted instead. She went back to the spuds. I went up the stairs and I could smell Rosko when she started talking to herself at the sink.

They used a saw and a big pair of scissors to get the plaster off. My arm had shrunk in the cast; the other one was much thicker by the side of it. The skin was peeling into lots of yellowish flakes. There was this musty smell, not the same smell as I thought rooks had, but a stale musty, like an air raid shelter. They said it had taken such a long time to mend because the fracture was complicated. That's what they said. I looked down at my arm lying on the table, not even daring to try a finger because the whole thing looked dead without the cast. And the arm didn't seem like mine anymore; there was no weight in it I could feel. I wanted to scratch at the flakes, scrape that smell away, and stop the itch they said would go when the plaster came off, but hadn't. I thought about climbing Rosko's rope and wondered would I ever be able to again. They talked about "it" all the time, as if the poorly arm wasn't part of me, as if my arm was separate, like a doll's arm you can take off. They said it needed "physio." Another funny word I didn't know, "physio." I wondered how would you spell that word, and thought like "fizz" in pop, with an "io" on the end like in radio.

When I asked the gatekeeper where to go for "physio" he pointed to a sign and told me to follow the ones like it. I felt a right idiot when I saw it. My "fizzio" was nowhere near theirs. And then there was the "therapy" bit on the end they never said. The next morning as I walked by the gatekeeper I remembered how he'd pointed and said, follow signs same as that there. And I realized he'd pointed because he thought I couldn't read. I never looked up at him again.

On my second Monday back in school I waited over by the tree where Rosko always stands but when the bell went to go in he hadn't come. I looked back as I went through the doors to see if he was running but he never came.

I pleaded with Joan in break, and in the end she said she would go to his house and ask for him, but not before I'd told her what I promised my mum, that I wouldn't have no more to do with Rosko. She said she'd never been to his house before and it would seem fishy. What if the man there was nasty or something? I said she could say she was asking after him for friends in school. She said he had no friends except me. I said the man wouldn't know that and anyway his mum might answer. She said she was scared. I told her there was nothing to be scared

of she was being a sissy. Then she said all right she'd
think of something if she hadn't run off by the time they
came to the door.

She did it. Next day she told me the man came to the
door, said Rosko was poorly, and shut it in her face. She
said he had a plaster over his ear. And she told me next
time do my own dirty work.

We were doing writing. I was back with my right hand.
Joan was sitting next to me and Miss Carter was up the
front at her desk writing something too. I still felt like
jumping on her sometimes but I didn't because she'd
given me the extra lessons and because I was really too
big to be doing it anymore. There was a knock at the
door. Everyone looked up. Miss Carter went over. This
policeman came in carrying his flat hat and a stick. His
chin was just a fold in his neck. He said something to
Miss Carter we couldn't hear properly; "missing" I picked
out. Something had been stolen, I thought, perhaps from
her and he'd come about it. Must be important anyway
because only high-up police have flat hats and sticks.
They stopped talking before I could make anything else
out. He gave a little bow and left. Miss Carter told us it
was none of our business and if the work wasn't finished
by the bell we would have to stay behind until it was.

"Oh Miss," we all moaned.

This time I saw it. Next day. I was throwing some bits
of paper from my satchel in the bucket under the sink.
"MISSING." In great big letters on the newspaper stuffed
in there. She'd put it there to stop me seeing, maybe to
stop him too. But he always asked for the paper when he
came in so what was she going to tell him, I wondered.

I unfolded it: "BOY GOES MISSING." Underneath it said, his mother says he's never done this before, never gone missing, he's a good boy, please if anybody knows anything. . . . They were going to bring dogs to search if he'd not been found by the weekend. The photo looked nothing like Rosko. There was a telephone number. I thought should I ring and say, "He's in the dingle," and run off. But I didn't know how to use a phone and anyway I'd promised not to tell. Then I thought, Rosko can look after himself, he'll be all right.

"Hazel, you there?"

"Yes, Mum."

I had the paper folded again but she'd caught me with it.

"You know then."

"Rosko's run."

She put her bag down. She looked down at the paper in my hand.

"They'll find him," she said.

"Do they always?"

"Most times."

"What'll they do if they catch him?"

"Take him home."

"But 'e's run from there."

"Dunner matter, he's under age."

"Do you —"

"He's not old enough to leave home."

"He'll run again."

"Hazel. You promised. Forget about him. He's up to no good. If your dad —"

"But Mum."

"I want hear no more about it. Give me that paper."

She went over to the sink with it, and I went upstairs and shut my door.

I kept it behind the picture of Jesus. It was safe there. It was nearly full of writing now. I started doing it because of Miss Carter. She told me I was good in English (she made us call it that and not "reading and writing" anymore) and I should try hard. I wanted her to like me so I thought if I practiced in a diary as well as in school I'd get better. But soon I got to like doing it just for me. I did it most nights when I was safe from him. I used an old exercise book I found in the store cupboard one day when it was my turn to hand out pencils. Miss Carter said I could have it without even asking me what I wanted it for. But soon I would have to get another one from somewhere.

I want Rosko to come back. I could see him without them knowing. I like him. I miss you Rosko. I think about him all the time. Brian Valant called Jane Phillips a silly cow to her face today. She scratched his face and ran off. Miss Carter was not in school. They said she'd gone for an exam. Why? She's a teacher. They know everything. My dad is a wall. He has broken glass on top. Wish he weren't my dad. He isn't really. He is always horible to my mum. He's getting worse. Why can't we get rid of him? Rosko doesn't have a dad, Joan found out. We dont need one either. Hope you're there Rosko because I'm going to bring you some food when they go to sleep. I promised mum I wouldn't see you again. She made me. I wont tell on the hut. You know I wont. When I was little I went shopping with my mum once. Granma went to. In the shop there was a pile of jars of lemon curd one on top of another like a triangle. I took one from the bottom without one on top of it. I got the lid off and put my finger in and licked. This boy saw me from behind some boxes. He called the manager. He said mum had to pay for it. She tried not to but he told her he was going to call police. Granma said I was wicked. She was going to tell my dad. I shivered. For ages every day I waited to be hit for the lemon curd. But he never hit me for it so mum must have got granma not to tell on me. When she was alive she was for ever telling on me.

I put it back behind Jesus. I got into bed with my clothes on and waited for Mum and Graham to go to bed but I fell asleep waiting. When I woke it was dark and still but I didn't know what time it was so I waited for the church clock. I counted twelve chimes. It was safe to go. I tiptoed down the stairs. I couldn't remember which one creaked loud and I hit it and froze, expecting one of them to catch me, but the night came back quiet and I got to the kitchen without doing any more creaks.

The kitchen clock was louder than daytime, and the tap dripped with every other tick. I fumbled in the larder over jars and tins and in boxes. I put some cheese and oatcakes in a bag with some little currant buns from Mum's Tuesday bake. They never locked the back door. The latch was heavy, I let it down slow as I could. I started to remember the way: the turns, the woods, the fields, the fences, the river, the ups and downs. I hoped I could go right.

There were some holes in the clouds. The moon was big. When it poked through it was much easier to go.

Getting to the copse with the copper beeches was quick.
I stopped where the old stables used to be, that burned
down with horses in, in a fire some say was started deliberate to get revenge on Mr. Binkley, the horse breeder.
Now all that was left were charred posts sticking out of
the field. I tried to go over the way from here in my head
and remembered we went down the bluff next. I skipped
down the long slope over the cattle paths to the river.
Rosko said it was the same river where much further
along, near the bridge with the passing places on it, we
fished for bullnoggers with jam jars, and tried to catch
little elvers with our bare hands. We never did. I stood
close to the water, which tinkled and lisped over the black
stones, and then the moon polished the water, made it
shine and some of the stones changed color and winked
at the water. Not-me in the water looking at me; me
looking at not-me in the water; but when the moon
stopped polishing we couldn't change places because we
both disappeared. An owl screeched and I splashed and
something scampered over my feet at the edge. With a
foof the owl was gone. We had scared each other and
between us we scared the little creature on the ground.
It was all right for them they belonged to the night. I
tried not to be frightened and remembered what Rosko
said about the dingle. I crossed two more fields and got
to the lane. I climbed into the field across the other side
and hoped it was the one with the dingle. It was. The
gaps in the clouds were bigger now but his gate was still
hard to find. I went past it a few times. I put the bag of
food inside the fence as far as I could reach without going

in, and I tried to hide it from my side by piling up some loam and twigs. I ran back to the lane and was glad to be over the hedge. Whatever Rosko said the dingle was really scary. I thought if he didn't find the food the animals in there would, before the dogs came sniffing after him.

The dogs smelled them under some gorse at Leggits' Deep: shoes, socks, trousers with an S-belt, shirt, and a green pullover with holes in it. His mother said they were what he was wearing and the police took them away to look for clues. They were the clothes he always had on. Frogmen went down the old mine shaft but came up with nothing but some sheep bones. They dredged a pond. Rosko wasn't there. They asked for him on the radio and it was in all the papers. Everyone was talking about it, making up horrid stories of what had happened to him. But no Rosko. Before long the police admitted they were baffled and had no new leads. There had been no reports of the boy from anywhere and they could find no body. By then people had stopped talking about him and there was nothing in the papers anymore.

Leggits' Deep was a long way from the dingle. He's alive, I kept telling myself. He's alive, safe in his hut. Then one day I couldn't believe he was and I stopped looking for him in the playground, stopped hearing him call me from bushes, stopped smelling him on my pillow. But it wasn't the same without him. I was miserable. Then a few weeks later just before I fell asleep I was smelling him in my room again and after that I never let him go. We did things together and he became today and tomorrow again, and sometimes when Joan said "Why you smiling?" I lied so as not to tell on Rosko.

Marge Toomin said she had been in the man's house and he had given her some sweets and some money and if I went he would give me some too. She said he said he liked me and had seen me skipping in the lane. I never saw him watching. She lived right the other end of the lane, near the road. She'd only just started coming this far down and talking to me. I don't know what made her (unless it was the man) because none of her friends lived down our end, and I never liked her in school. She was a year older than me.

The man lived in the last house, where the lane stopped. It was a house like ours but he never opened the curtains even when the sun was out, and his garden was full of tall weeds, and dandelions grew from the cracks in the concrete path up to his front door. He was quite old. Not very old. His hair was greasy, plastered down.

Marge Toomin never stopped talking about boys. "You've got to get a boyfriend," she kept saying. "If you don't," she said, "there's something wrong with you." All her friends had boys and she told me they all said it's no good without one. She said lots of boys liked her and why didn't any like me, where was mine. One of her friends got a magazine off her big sister and in it, she told me, were love stories, and a page about how to get boys if you were having trouble finding them. She went on and on about them. She tried to persuade me to go to the man's house with her. I didn't want to and trying to get out of it said I would if she walked on the wet cement they had just laid in Jones's yard. She did it. But they caught her on the cement and she got in trouble and said it was me told her do it, dared her to, and Mr. Jones said it was her was caught, so it was her to blame, and Mrs. Jones came out and said she knew about her, everybody knew what a little liar she was, and she clipped her round the ear as she came off the cement and said she'd tell her mother and Marge ran then with blobs of cement falling off her shoes and shouted back she didn't give a monkey's who they told, then she turned and stuck her tongue out and ran off faster when Mr. Jones lurched forward like he was going to chase.

Next day she was back again. I was skipping. It was half-term from school. No one was at home. She asked me where my boyfriend was today. She said she'd seen hers this morning and was going to meet him later over Bears' Hollow. She wanted to know had I ever kissed a boy, had I ever let one put his hand down. She said she had. And laughed. I had to go the man's house now, she said, because she'd walked on Jones's yard.

She went first. We went round the back. I had my skipping rope wrapped round my arm. She said he left the back door open for her so she could come anytime and he never locked it even at night. He was sitting in the easy chair. I think we woke him up. In the corner a kettle hummed over a low light. The mugs on the drainer were like Rosko's. He had a can of Heinz mushroom soup open on the table, and a woman with no clothes on kneeling on a bed looked down at us from a calendar above the range.

He got up slow from the chair shuffling his feet. He

seemed to have trouble balancing at first. He looked at me (I felt he was, I was looking down) and said:

"You've fetch'd her then, Marge."

"Her didn't want come, though."

"Did you tell her about sweets, how many there are?"

"I told her."

"Plenty more where them come from, you know."

I was looking at him now. His eyes spurted nonstop from side to side like he was trying to see everything at once, even behind him. He had white whiskers. They grew in little clumps on his red face with empty spaces between them. His trousers were a mile too big for him. The room smelt a mixture of how Granma used to smell of pee, when she couldn't hold it anymore, and that camphorated oil Mum rubbed in my chest when I had a cough. Only his eyes were moving.

"Does your friend know what we do before we get sweets?"

"Just told her I got sweets and money like you said."

"Your name's Hazel, isn't it?"

"Yes."

"D'you like sweets?"

"Yes."

"We have do things first then we get sweets, don't we, Marge."

His voice was wobbly, not very loud. He pointed at the cupboard.

"Show her sweets, Marge. We have to promise not to tell. It's a secret what we do. We don't want anything nasty to happen, do we, if we tell. I don't want to have to get . . . Fetch sweets, Marge. If you're really good you get a sixpence and all."

Marge went to the cupboard and pulled out a big cocoa tin. I watched him most. I thought, As long as he stays there I'll be safe.

"Show Hazel all the sweets, Marge."

She prized the lid off with a spoon handle and holding the tin in both hands pushed it under my nose. There were lots of sweets, humbugs too, my favorite. It was full almost to the top.

"Let's show Hazel what we do for sweets and a sixpence, Marge."

She put the tin down heavy on the table; the toffee wrappers rustled and the humbugs jankled, like money does if you shake a piggy bank. She brushed by me and I turned sideways so I could still see her and watch him. She locked the door. A grubby net curtain hung from a wire over the window. The corners of the room were dark. I stayed near the door and thought, What if he makes us go in the front where the curtains are always closed, where it'll be dark. But she went over to him where he was, where he'd not moved from, where he must be most of his time (except sitting, not standing), where she began to rub herself against him. He was not much taller than her. She rubbed harder after a bit and the bottom of his mouth fell down and he grunted through the hole it left, quiet ones at first, then louder. She started to rub his trousers with her hand about the same place where I'd seen Rosko's things, when I saw the difference the first time. He sighed and slumped into the chair. She followed him down and kept rubbing. She pulled his zipper open, which ran over his belly like a railway track over a hill, and put her hand in there and moved it around. She lifted her dress with her other hand and pulled her knickers down and held her dress up while he put his hand under and rubbed. She pulled out the thing from his trousers. It stuck up a bit bendy and she had her hand round it rubbing up and down and he carried on doing it to her. He looked up at me, his eyes still spurting, and said:

"C'mon, Hazel, it's your turn now."

I shuddered. My heel was touching the door.

"I like you, luv, c'mon. It's nice in your knickers, you'll see."

She started doing it faster to him. I fumbled behind me to get the door open. He moaned. I saw this white stuff dribble from the end of it onto her hand and I turned and ran, clutching at my rope. I sat on our step panting, fearing him, fearing he'd come after me.

When she came by I was sitting in the same place making shadows with my rope, dangling it in the sun, seeing the old man's eyes flounce in and out of them leering at me, and the eyes stayed there even if I stopped making shadows.

She was angry with me and told me never to tell anyone, else she would tell my dad. She said I could have had sweets and a sixpence. She shouted back from down the lane:

"You'll never get boys if you keep runnin' off like that."

Like Mum said he would Graham went down pit. At Fendon Colliery. He never came home dirty. He scrubbed in the pithead baths until every last speck was off him. He didn't say anything (not to me) but I knew he hated it at the pit. He wanted no black on him, to remind him, after he walked out the gates, no black for others to know by. Mum put his box ready for him: some sandwiches, a piece of cake or a bun, and tea; he had a separate little bottle with a screw cap for the milk. In his mean way he'd forced Graham to get a job at a different colliery from where he worked, and Uncle Sid used to. He didn't want Graham working with him. I think because he couldn't stand the thought of Graham being a better miner because he was young and healthy. Every week Graham paid Mum out of his wages. As soon as he came in with his packet he opened it in the kitchen, picking at the brown paper trying not to tear it. It excited him seeing the money; just then he seemed to forget his misery. But when he was too hasty he ripped the notes and that got him annoyed. He put the change in his pocket. I hoped he'd give me some, a penny or two, but he never did. One week he gave Mum more than he was supposed to and asked her to save it for him. She told him he could buy savings certificates at the post office; that way his money would grow.

Soon after Graham started saving he gave his rabbit away, not Hopper, he was dead, but another one called Clive, to a boy who lived down the lane near Marge Toomin's house. The boy had a doe and was looking for a Dutch buck to go with it. The boy tried to give Graham some money for the buck but Graham said he didn't want any. Graham, I was pretty sure, thought it made him a grown-up somehow, not taking money. Stupid if you ask me 'cause money is what they were always talking about, saying they never had enough, and there he was giving

it away. Since he'd started down Graham acted funny,
as if half of him said no to what he was, a miner now,
and the other half told him he had to get used to it. I
think that's why he got all confused about growing up
and didn't know what to do.

Graham told Mum he was going to get some racing
pigeons off a fancier from Fendon. When I heard him
tell her that I knew for certain he thought rabbits were
for boys. He said the man, Burt French, was going to
show him what to do and let him have some young birds
at a good price. Mum told him she wanted no mess and
where was he going to keep the bloody things. He told
her he wouldn't be bringing any birds home, not yet
awhile, because Burt said he could use his loft, as he had
more room than he needed now he'd cut down on his
stock birds; that way they could share the price of corn
and take turns guarding the loft when a big race was near.
He said Burt won prizes with his birds.

When Mum started getting me to help her a lot around
the house with dusting and all I knew it was because she
thought it was time now for me to know about house-
keeping and things.

I was helping her do the tea one day. Graham was at
the colliery on his shift. Dirty him was by the range
looking at the paper, a fag dangling out of his mouth,
smoke all in his hair. It started while I was looking at
him. He coughed and coughed again and he couldn't
stop. His chest shook. His eyes came forward like he was
being strangled. Don't let go, strangle him, I thought.
But he stopped before she slapped his back, before the

blood fell over his lip, clotted. The dark blob rolled down his chin until the coal dust on his face sucked it dry. She fetched a cloth from the sink and wiped it away. It left a white place where it had been, surrounded by black. He was quiet. She must have pretended he was someone else so she could be kind to him and help him. He sat there staring, trying to breathe without starting it up again. She ran the cold tap over the cloth and when it was only water going down the drain she turned it off.

That night it started again after we'd all gone to bed. You could hear everything through the walls in our house. It woke me up, his coughing.

"You'll have go doctor's —"

"Shut it, woman."

"You know it's your lungs what's —"

"Shut it, I said. I's going to no doctors."

"You know it's bad. It's —"

"For fuck's sake leave off, will yer."

"It'll only get worse if you don't."

I heard him strike her. She cried. He told her shut up moaning and open her legs if she wanted do something useful. I listened to the springs going and I shuddered. He went on coughing into the night. Early morning I heard the miners go by talking, then I heard him slam the door and scrape along behind them in the dark, coughing.

He came home coughing. We soon got used to it like we did when Granma came to live with us, like we did when she started to smell.

With all the leaves unfolded I couldn't see the old man's house from ours. If Marge Toomin was still do-

ing things for sweets and sixpence I didn't know. I never
saw her go past our house anyway. In school if she
saw me she gave me this look as if to say: you mardy
cow, you don't know what you'm missin'. The air was
moist, warm; little animals scurried around, the heat
making them go faster. As I walked back from school
the old blackbird with one leg was turning over some
rotten leaves at the side of the lane, looking for food,
trying not to fall over, flapping his wings now and again
to steady himself when he prodded too hard with his
beak.

I stopped by the dirty mirror at the end of the driveway
to the big house. When people lived there they used it
to see if it was clear to drive out into the lane. The last
person to live there was an old lady who never spoke to
anyone. I never saw her. Nobody did, I don't think.
When they broke in, so the story went, because she hadn't
paid any bills for a long time, they found her bones
waiting in a chair dressed in her best to go out, her velvet
hat still in place on her head, and thousands of pounds
in a bag on her knee.

I wrote *Rosko xxx* in the dust with my finger and I saw
some of my face reflected in the letters. It was lopsided.
Using two fingers at once I made the letters bigger. Now
more of me was there, but still lopsided, and whatever
way I put my head the mirror had me twisted.

"You been gone a long time now, Rosko," I said.

When I felt it I looked down. Blood on my leg. I
touched it. It was warm. With what was on my finger I
did an *H* after the *xxx*. *Rosko kiss kiss kiss Hazel*. Then
I dabbed more on my finger for the *S* but the dirt dried

it up so I dabbed more to finish it with. I kept going over the letters until they were red on the glass.

It'd come like she said it could, without any warning. I stuffed some dry grass down me to stop it up and pulled some more to wipe my leg with. A mistle thrush bobbed up, stopped, eyed me over, flicking its head all the time, then with a shake turned and bobbed down the bank towards the empty house. Must have thought it was a worm I pulled up. A beam of sun squeezed through between the larches, and the motes it lit up danced and reeled round the new green on the branches, some fast, some slow, disappearing then coming back, then going again. I said it over and over: Rosko loves H.S. Rosko loves H.S. Rosko loves H.S. When the words on the mirror began to blur I looked down between my knees where black ants struggled in the grass to carry bits and pieces much bigger than they were.

I blurted it out. It was stupid but I looked round at first, pretended someone else had said it. I cradled my knees. When the heat went out of my neck and face I said it out loud again:

"He did do that to you. He did."

I said it almost as easy as Rosko loves H.S. I wasn't afraid now.

Was it the blood? No. The blood's nothing to do with me. Like she said it would, it came with no warning, when it was ready. I cringed when I looked at it; knowing now. Come from the pit. His razor. The door pushed shut behind me after I'd run to him when he shouted. Click. The towel over his shoulder. The razor glaring. The smell of booze on his breath in the bathroom. The cold floor pressed up at me. I felt it before he touched. Butterfly belly squirming. Then the forcing. Locked down. Repeated against me. Stinging. The light burned my eyes but they wouldn't close. Until his moaning ended it.

The lane was very quiet when I walked back home. Everything was still. I opened the door slowly and stood on the step, waiting. I didn't have a shadow. She looked up from the sink.

"Bloody 'ell, what's 'appened?"

"Nothing."

"You're covered in dirt. You all right? Look at your face. Dirt's everywhere."

"Yeah."

"You're filthy. Look at you. Your clothes."

"I —"

"They're ruined. Come here. Let's get you out of them."

"No."

"Don't be daft."

"I hate him."

"Who? Who did it?"

"You know."

"Hazel, if you won't tell me how can I do —"

"What's there to do."

"What d'you mean?"

"I hate 'im."

"This'll never come clean in a month of Sundays. Wait till I catch who done it. Lift your arms up. What's this grass doing here?"

"The blood come. It's for that."

"Come by sink. I'll never get this out. Hurry up, I dunner want him finding you like this."

"I hate him."

"Hold you mouth."

"No. I hate him."

"Ssh. He could hear you."

"I don't care."

"It's all in you curls. C'mon, bend over. Close your eyes. There. Jus' got rinse it. Here, use this one for your 'air. I'll go get you some clean clothes and summat for the blood. Dry yourself proper."

She came back with the things, hurrying.

"Hazel. You didn't dry yourself. What's the matter with you."

She snatched the towel from round me and began to rub, pushing me so I had to keep moving my feet to balance.

"Here, hold this. Gimme that."

She grabbed the dry towel off me and did my hair with it, rubbing hard, buffeting almost, and I could see stars and little lights in my head.

"Put your clothes on quick. I'll get you a cardie. Don't want you catchin' cold."

She hurried off again then hurried back with my pink cardigan. She knew I liked it better than the navy one.

"Here, Hazel."

"I don't care."

"Stop that. I'll put kettle on. D'you want a biscuit?"

"Don't care."

She looked at me hard.

"I'll have one," I said.

She put some hot water in to warm the pot, swished

it round, emptied it down the drain, counted in three scoops of tea, and waited for the kettle to boil.

"They shouldn't do what they done to you and get away with it."

The kettle whistled. She filled the pot, put the cozy on and fetched the biscuits and sugar from the cupboard.

"Were he from your school?"

She gave me a biscuit, a ginger, and took one herself. Like always we dunked them in our tea. She was mad with me but was trying not to lose her temper.

"Are you coverin' for someone?"

"No."

"That Rosko isn't back?"

"No. I rubbed soil on me, rolled in it."

"You'm lying, Hazel."

"I'm not, God's honor."

She began to worry her face, pulling at her skin as if she was trying to peel off a mask.

"Can I have another biscuit?"

"Here."

"Ta."

"Did anyone see you?"

"No."

"What's got in you? Ruining your clothes like that. You think I'm made of money. God knows I work hard enough for it."

"Dunno."

"Dunno. Who does then. Never heard anything so bloody daft. Rubbin' dirt all over yourself."

"I don't care."

"HAZEL."

She slapped my face.

"Get out. I dunner want no more do with you till you get some sense back in your head."

My eyes watered over and I was running out of the kitchen before she could say any more.

For a long time the clap of my feet and the clap of my feet some more on the hard meadow, and the swish swish as they cut against the buttercups and grass and clover, and the broken strap of my sandal flapping, and the buckle going *tink tink*, was all there was.

The water didn't make a noise as it fell over the stones and whirled. Not then. Not when I first got to it.

I heard the clock on the church first, strike the bell, and after the ringing finished the water noise came back. And then the gray wagtail, that had scurried up the shallows along the stream, said *tzissi tzissi*, and dipped its head and neck forward with every movement, as if it was agreeing with itself, as it flickered over the watery stones. It paid no attention to me while I sat still, and now and then it darted after an insect saying *tzissi tzissi*.

There's bullnoggers in there. I don't care. There are, you know. Don't care, I said. Stop that, Hazel. Not going tell you again. Plenty to catch. Big ones. Can't miss. Told you not to do that before, ain't I, you little bitch. Bullnoggers in jam jars going round and round, head and tail, making fish eyes at you and you poking back at them to make them jump. I don't care anymore. She don't like you doin' it, do she. Come here, Hazel, I want you fer summat. No don't no no.

I leaned over the water. The wagtail had stopped picking at the river limpet it wanted from the stone, and was
flitting, up and down, like horses go on a merry-go-round,
the sulphur yellow on its breast flashing over the water.
I put my head under. Opened my eyes. Everything the
wrong way like in the mirror. Bended edges. Under more,
where it was tangled I saw him lurking in the mud, the
towel over his shoulder. And her with her words there
too, saying, You've got to work hard. . . . You've got
it in you if only . . . It'd be a shame to let it go to
waste. . . . When I tried to jump on her my feet wouldn't
let go of the ground. Rosko was there then, curved in
the weed. The cold water ran down my back and down
my front onto my breasts and my nipples went tight and
tingled and my face was numb and my eyes and mouth
stayed shut. I put my head back in, deeper. I opened
them again but nothing would wash away. The towel.
And him. Ready to do it to me again. And her at her
desk, her glasses slid down her nose, reciting the words
almost, then spelling them out once, then twice. And
Rosko lying there, rotting, small fishes sheltering in the
holes in him, only their gills moving, while the weeds
held him back, for the water to run over him, rub him
to bone; and when I went to loose him when he called,
pieces of his pale lips broke off and were swept away
before I could touch him. I tried again but the weeds
lifted him away now so I couldn't reach. And the wagtail
came back and landed on him, spreading and lifting its
tail like a fan, displaying its coverts, and then it pecked
after something in one of the holes in his back and said
tzissi tzissi. I thrashed both arms to scare it but under

the water it wasn't afraid of me, and every time I got near
Rosko the weeds moved him away. The water went dark.
She got up from the desk and turned her back on me
and walked away and threw my book down. The pages
came out and floated to where he stood and he stamped
on them until every page was buried under the mud.
The ink came off and made a cloud in the water. Then
he came after me, snarling, but Rosko was lying in the
way. He dropped the towel over Rosko's head and slashed
his way through him with the rusting razor, cut him in
half, and a shoal of tiny fishes came out of him and swam
round, keeping in the red water. He waded through them,
chopping at them as he came to get at me.

"You all right, missy? Missy. You all right? Don't be
afraid, I won't hurt you. This is no place for sleeping."
I smelled him first; like a shippon that's had no cattle
in it for a long time, that's cobwebbed and piled high
with bags of animal feed. Before I opened my eyes I
wanted to touch him. He smelled safe.
His hair was fine and white, and curled. Nearly all the
whiskers sticking out of his face were white too. The few
dark ones made him look a bit mean. But when he smiled
I saw where his teeth used to be and he didn't look mean
with all soft gums showing.
"You're wet right through. Here."
He helped me up. He held my hand gentle. The skin
on his hand was hard.
"What you doin' here?"
"Nothing."
"Funny place for doing nothing this time o' morning."

He smiled. It pushed his nose up.

"You was sound asleep when I seen you. That isn't doing nothing. If you ask me I'd say you's run off. When dark come you was so wore out with running and worrying you cried yoursen to sleep. Let's get you up there where it's a bit warmer."

I said nothing. We had to scramble up the small bank into the meadow because it started to give way under us as soon as we started up it. When I looked back to see where I'd slept the stream was vanished in the mist. The mist covered the field too and poked in the hedgerows, hovering and pushing about, impatient, as if it had lost something.

"You sure you're all right?"

"Yeah."

"When sun gets up proper you'll dry pretty quick. You can 'ave this coat if you's cold."

"I'm all right."

"Mustn't forget these little beauties."

His back to me, he bent down near the trunk of a dead elm and pulled them out of the mist. Two pheasants and a hare. Tied up. Limp. The heads of the birds flopped together, upside down, like puppets with broken strings. Fresh dead blood dripped from their beaks, from one then the other, and the hare hung with them, upside down, its eyes still open, blood clotted in its nostrils and one of its front paws severed. He threw them over his shoulder. They moved like a jacket would have. Some blood came out of them and made a thin line, and it fell through the mist in an arc.

"What they call you, missy?"

"Hazel."

I smelled him again. I'd forgotten then for a minute. I must have. The smell seemed it was there a long time. That he had been too. I smelled him again on purpose. We saw a rabbit run into a patch of mist.

"There's one I could have 'ad," he said.

I couldn't smell the animals behind his back and wondered how long before I would, and whether birds rotted faster than furry things.

"Hazel. That were her name, me mother's. God rest her soul. Where you from?"

"Village over there."

I pointed back where the river was.

"There's a lot on 'em over there. I ought know, I've been round these parts for over seventy year. Which side of the Trent?"

"Is that there the River Trent?"

"Was yesterday. You know it starts less than a mile up there, underground."

He smiled as he pointed.

"Never knew that were Trent. Thought it —"

"You do now."

"It's over the far side then, the village is."

"Which one the other side?"

"One with a spire."

"Got me work cut out here, I can see. Can think of three easy with spires. Fratton?"

"No."

"Gorton then?"

"No."

"Here, it's got be Riddon Moor then."

"No it 'asn't."

"I give up."

"One more."

"Give us a clue."

"Steeple's a bit —"

"Crooked. Grebedown. Stone me. Why didn't I think of that straight off. Digged me a grave there once. When sexton were on panel with phlebitis a man I knowed put me on to it. Vicar, funny fella he was, liked his tipple mind, said I could have the job if I weren't taphophobic. Told him I'd nothing against the Welsh and he laughed and gave me the job. Never could figure what them vicar fellas were on about half the time. Pie-in-the-sky stuff if you ask me. Was a backbreaker. Sandy soil. Weighs a ton. You have to use lining boards to stop the bugger caving in. Vicar come along when I done digging. Said I'd done boards wrong for putting 'em upright. They was meant to be lengthways. I done 'em like when I were navvying. Had to give up the navvying on account of me wheezes. Mourners wouldn't be able to see the coffin, he said. They liked to get a last look at the coffin. It was the one they remembered most, he said, when it was all the way in the ground. So I changed 'em. That were the last grave I digged. One were enough. Drank the proceeds in the Cock and Turtle. Six feet's a lot further down than you think."

"My uncle Sid's buried there. And me granma."

"I wouldn't mind being buried in Cock an' Turtle."

He laughed and I saw his shiny gums again. We pushed through a gap in the hedge. He went first, them animals swaying across his back.

"You must be hungry."

"Am a bit."

"You like mushrooms?"

"They're all right."

"I know where we'll get some. I's got summat good to go with them and all. A real treat."

Sweets, I thought. Sweets. I can run faster than him, he's old. I'll wait until he's not looking and beat it back over the river. Once I'm on the bluff he'll never get me. He was looking at me. He smiled like he knew he'd frightened me. I watched him, remembered the smell, and smelled him again.

"What treat?"

"Wait-and-see-treat. Let's get mushrooms first."

The sun was up now and things were beginning to dry. I felt warmer as my clothes began to steam a little. We followed a cow path across. Not very far along it he stopped me all of a sudden.

"Ssh. Listen."

I heard: *chit-chit, chit-chit.*

"What bird's that?"

"Yellowhammer. I can't see it but that's what it is all right. Sometimes they sit on top of hedge and sing. Little-bit-of-bread-and-No-cheese, it sounds like. The devil's bird."

I could only hear *chit-chit.*

"Little-bit-of-bread-and-No-cheese," he said again as he started walking.

"Why's it called devil's bird?"

" 'Cause of the writing on its eggs. People thought it

brought 'em bad luck. They used to smash the eggs. Some call it the writing lark."

"Does it bring bad luck?"

"I don't know, I could never read the writing."

After a few strides he pulled the bag off his shoulder and swung the animals round to the front, and changed them over. I moved to the side with the bag. The yellowhammer was quiet. We went towards the corner of the field.

"Over there," he said.

As he lowered his arm the bag strap came off his shoulder. He caught it before I could.

"I knowed they'd be there."

"How'd you know?"

"They was here yesterday. I knowed if it stayed warm and a bit moist there'd be more today."

As he lowered the animals to the ground their necks bent double and the weight of their bodies coming after pinned them like that. They were a shambles now, crumpled bloody feathers, broken wings, and legs splayed out lame as stones.

"Why you staring?"

"Them animals," I said.

"What's wrong with 'em?"

"They aren't much cop like that."

He bent down to pick mushrooms. He'd picked a few when he looked up.

"You royalty or summat?"

"I were just —"

I crouched down fast and began to pick. The smile was back on his face.

"Take no notice on me, I were only kidding."

The mushrooms were big across so we soon had enough. He ate the stalk off one of them.

"They grow big fast," I said.

"When conditions is favorite there's no stopping 'em."

He pulled a square of faded white cloth from his bag and spread it on the ground and weighted it with a stone because a breeze had started. He put the ones he'd picked on it, blowing an insect off one of them first, and I put mine next to his. I hadn't done so bad. He tied a knot with them when he'd pulled the corners together.

"That should take care of them till we's ready," he said.

He gave me the bundle of mushrooms to carry. He collected up his animals and shuffled the bag strap over the little humps in the shoulder of his jacket, bent his knees, then flicked them straight. That seemed to get everything comfortable, after the load had jogged up and flopped down in a different place on his back. His jacket went almost down to his knees and it was a wonder it held together, it needed patches so bad. He rolled the sleeves over at the cuffs because they were too long. The striped lining was worn and yellowed and in some places on it there were dried blood marks.

"There's a place right near where I stops for a bite to eat when I work this neck of the woods," he said.

I followed him over the stile into the next meadow, holding the bundle high as I could so as not to bump the mushrooms on the wooden bars. The mist had nearly all gone. We stuck close by the hedge. He went faster now, touching the ground lightly as if he was trying not to be heard. A tiptoe walk almost. Who was going to hear him, I thought. There was only me. And then I thought with legs light as that maybe I wouldn't beat him on the bluff. I kept in behind him like he told me and looked at the ground all the time so I didn't have to watch them animals bob and roll on his back. Without warning the field went very steep, away from us.

"There's the river down there," I said. "We've come a long way round."

"Had get mushrooms."

"But it's still a long way round."

"Them pastures we skirted what butts on river back there is dangerous. I never touches 'em."

"Why they dangerous? Me and my friend Rosko used go in fields round here. Never had no trouble. Except once we had a fight with some boys from another village who were killing our butterflies. But that weren't field's fault, were it. They made our noses bleed but we chased 'em off."

"Good for you."

"Why they dangerous then?"

"For them in my profession they is."

"What's that?"

"You don't need telling."

He could catch me every time. I wanted him to tell me about poachers but I knew he wouldn't now so I shut up. He started to go even quicker than before, fidgeting as he went, but not on tiptoe anymore. He took thick deliberate strides, the heels and the soles of his boots flattening the grass as they came down. I kept my place behind, minding the mushrooms and marching after him, imitating him. At the bottom of the steep he managed to stop all of a sudden. I bumped into him.

"Steady up there, old gal," he said.

"Sorry, I weren't watchin' where I were going."

I would have hit him if I had been watching he stopped so dead on the steep.

"Be careful gettin' through here," he said. "There's thorns and it's a bit of a squeeze."

He pushed through the gap in the hedge sideways. One of the birds got caught. He tugged at it. Pulled it loose. Which left a lot of feathers behind. Some stayed in the hedge spiked next to the leaves and some spun round free in the air. He waited for me to come through. When I got to his side he turned to go on and I saw that the bird had had one of its eyes ripped out in the tug. I tried not to think about it, but I did anyway; what good's a dead eye in a dead bird? After I thought different, but just as stupid, maybe even a dead bird's better off with its eyes in.

He stopped at the edge of the bank and looked down at the stream, watched it from right and left, then stood still looking some more before he unloaded himself, taking the animals off first. They went down like before, necks bent double.

"We're pretty safe here. Cover all round. If we hear anyone we just wades over yonder. That's common ground."

I looked where he meant but I couldn't see beyond the trees, they made such a dense screen. They grew hard against the bank so over that side there was nowhere secret to sit. The only place you could see out from was up, where the sky was all blue now, where the sun would burn through onto our little patch, once it got over the treetops.

"Keep your eye on 'em," he said. "I'll be back in a tick."

"Where you goin'?"

"Get some kindling."

"Can I come help?"

"Dunner see why not. These can watch 'emselves for a bit."

He laid his bag on top of the animals and took the mushrooms off me and put them by the bag.

"Will mushrooms be all right to eat if they've touched dead —"

"Make 'em taste better, will that. Dunner worry. Let's get that kindling."

After the fire was started and he'd told me that only very dry tinder was any good to use because it made no smoke, and he'd taken a small fry pan from his bag and a mug and a tin flask, he said:

"Haven't forgot treat, you know. Wait here this time. You'll be all right."

When he'd disappeared down the bank I watched the fire burn but soon I was staring only at the heap of animals. Was him. Stepping out of the carcasses roaring after me and I was running backwards now. Not the razor but a butcher knife chopping at the air. And I turned to see if he was behind me coming to get me that way too and Mum was there with a bag of dusters and a broom and her hair tied in a scarf and she said to come home it would be all right there was nothing to worry over

anymore and I turned and he was stepping out of the
carcasses scraping bits of the flesh off him with the back
of the knife and the hare winked at me from down there,
its eye all cloudy, and I heard it say, "Never go back,
Rosko didn't."

"Here we have it. Did I scare you?"

"A bit. Never heard you comin'. What's that?"

Before he said anything I looked at the hare and back.
Its eye was closed.

"What I went for."

"But it's a ball of mud."

"That's only part of it."

He went down on one knee and placed the ball gently
in the fire. Some of the mud stuck to his hands. The fire
was fierce red now and he rolled hot embers up around
the mud ball with a stick he'd kept back from the wood
we'd collected.

"Cook quick in there," he said. "Want some tea?"

"Yes please."

"Here."

It was dirtier on the inside than Rosko's mugs, dark
brown, almost black. It was enamel just the same. We
passed it to one another and when it was empty he filled
it from his flask without spilling a drop and we drank that
one too. He pulled some rounds of bread from a Mother's
Pride wrapper he'd fumbled out of his bag on the ground
behind him while he was poking with the stick at the
embers. The rounds had dripping on. He took a slice and
rubbed the side with dripping on around the fry pan and
the bread broke and he picked the bits out and ate them
and some crumbled more and those bits fell on the grass

where ants struggled to take them away. He told me he
had bread and dripping every day even if he had nothing
else, and it was best with salt sprinkled on, and he asked
me if I liked it and I said I did but I'd only eaten it once
or twice, and he gave me a slice and said to sprinkle some
salt on mine from the little twist of blue paper he'd saved
from a crisp packet, so I did, and it tasted good and I
wasn't thinking of going back when the dripping spat out
of the pan and he threw the mushrooms in. He poked
at them to keep them from burning and then put the
stick in the fire, rolled the mud ball over in the embers
with it but left it there too long because it set alight and
when he'd banged it out on the grass he flicked at the
mushrooms with the end of it still smoking.

"There's another slice of dripping apiece," he said.
"Take one."

"What's your name?"

"They calls me Pockets."

"Thanks for the dripping, Pockets," I said.

I said "Pockets" louder than anything else. I liked it.
It was better than Graham, or Alan, or John, Pockets
was. And I thought not to ask him why they called him
Pockets because he'd only say I knew and catch me again.
So I had to think of ways of saying it without getting him
angry.

"How long you done this job, Pockets?" I said.

And that time he didn't know what I was up to. Well,
he never said he did.

"It were during Fourteen-Eighteen War I started. About
thirty-six year ago that would make it. They never sent
me to the front on account of me wheezin', and building

firm I were working for at the time folded. I were out of
work. I weren't really sorry for not having go fight but I
did fancy me chances against them German boys. 'Cause
I were on doctor's panel they overlooked me fer civilian
effort an' all. I were ducking and diving to make ends
meet when I bumps into this old geezer one day who
come from the north, and he got me started. Worked
together a few times and he learned me tricks of the trade,
night work an' all, and he said a million times if he ever
said it once, it were best thing for me wheezin' were
workin' in fresh air. Turned up one night, usual place,
to go after some trout but he never showed. Never seen
or heard on him again. Shit. Excuse me, miss. This here's
goin' be burnt to a cinder."

He took hold of the stick and stabbed the ball out from
the fire and left it smoldering on the grass, scorching it
and burning some ants. He put the mushrooms out of
the fire too.

"Now," he said. "What's fit for a king."

He opened the blade of the knife. It shone. It was worn
thin to a crescent shape with all the sharpening it'd had.
I trusted it. He drove the charred end of the stick hard
into the baked mud again. The blade sliced in easy and
he cut all the way round moving the ball a little at a time
with the stick then steadying it for the cut. After prizing
it with the back edge of the knife in a few places along
the cut the ball fell in two. There was meat in there
piping hot.

"What's that?"

"That's it. Gimme the plate."

I shook an ant off and gave it him.

"But what is it?"

He scooped some bits of meat on the plate pushing them to the side, some of the meat fell off the tiny bones, and he dolloped mushrooms in the middle covering the black spot where the enamel had chipped off.

"Get some down you while it's hot."

"But I —"

"What do it look like?"

"Meat."

"It's meat all right. You eat meat, don't yer?"

"Yeah."

"Well then."

He held the plate so we could both eat off it. He put his nose into the steam and sniffed deep, then started, meat, mushrooms, a bite of dripping, and he did it over like that.

"Cooked to a T," he said. "Better than one I had last week. Tough were that one."

I tried a piece, put some mushroom and bread in with it. I was still chewing and said:

"Tell us what it is."

"Hedgehog."

I spat it out. Some of it went in the fire and hissed.

"And what's up with 'edgehog?"

He took another piece of the stuff and chewed with delight.

"Best I've ever had. Forget about it's 'edgehog and you'll like it all right."

"But I never, didn't know you could 'ave it."

"First time you had mother's milk you didn't know neither. Like chicken?"

"Yeah."

"So what's up with 'edgehog."

I wanted to show him back so I put a piece in my mouth and thought Chicken, chicken, but the hedgehog wouldn't go down, and I gagged a few times before I managed to swallow it, thinking Now he'll kill me if I go back. I can't go back, I can't.

"Good, eh," he said.

"What 'appened to all its spines? I like hedgehogs."

"And me."

"I mean I —"

"They're in the mud. Mud bakes hard and traps the spines. When you pull the mud apart the spines pull the skin with 'em and you's left with the meat. Only road I know of skinning 'edgehog."

"Not eating no more. 'Edgehogs are nice animals."

"You don't like chickens so you eat them?"

"What you mean?"

"You're telling me you only eat things you don't like."

He laughed at me. I saw chewed meat sticking to his gums. He went back to chewing it and when he finished he was staring into the fire. I wished he wouldn't laugh at me like that. I looked back at his animals again.

"Rosko, you said he were called."

"Yeah. He were my best friend."

A wasp hovered near his mouth after the meat it could smell.

"Womit you ramol," he said flicking after it. "That were name of lad what went missing, Rosko."

"Yeah, that's him."

"Never found him, just them clothes."

"I know he's not dead."

"Weren't when they found his clothes."

"What you mean?"

"I were in dingle early one morning when I smells smoke."

"So?"

"Hut were empty when I found it, fire still goin'. Tea-pot were warm an' all. He must have heard me and scarpered. I's pretty quiet, I dunner know how he heard."

"How d'you know it were Rosko was in there?"

"I didn't till now."

"What you mean?"

" 'Cause it were your name carved in his table, fresh. Went back next day. No sign of him. He hadn't been back. That were a long time since."

"Why didn't you tell?"

"What were there to tell. Hut were empty. I'd have made a right fool of meself. Besides I didn't want 'em knowing I poached the dingle."

"You think he's alive?"

"Why shouldn't he be. Look'd like he knew how take care of hisself to me. You like the lad a lot."

"So?"

"Nothing. He'll come to no harm. Maybe one day —"

He stopped and began to prod his gums with his finger.

"You didn't finish," he said.

"I'm full."

"Not on that measly bit you aren't."

He threw the scraps of hedgehog on the fire then began gathering up his things.

"You haven't said anything about why you's run off."

"It's —"

"It'll be a secret with me, dunner worry."

"It's me dad."

"What about him?"

"He beats me and —"

"Does your mother —"

"He beats her an' all."

"That's bad. What you goin' do?"

"Dunno. Thought maybe you'd . . ."

"You ought go home. Be for best in long road. No place out here for, I mean, whatever 'appens I won't say a word."

"But I could come —"

"Them tears'll do you no good. If I take you with me they'll lock me up before you can say Jack Robinson. Listen, I'll tell you what, if you're still here tomorrow I'll fry up a right good breakfast. No 'edgehog, promise."

"You're just like him. I don't want go with you any-road."

"In mornin' then I'll be here. Got be gettin' along now, there's a man waiting for them there beauties."

"Please yourself."

He threw a piece of wood that was still smoldering into the river. I rubbed my eyes to see him better.

"Wonder if that'll reach Humber Estuary," he said.

"Who cares," I said loud.

He loaded himself, looked at me, pushed a smile across his mouth, and said:

"Taraa a bit."

With a shuffle and skip he was gone over the bank.

I stared at the place where he'd waded over, where it

was deep past his knees, with them animals bobbing once more on his back. I saw them all for a long time after they'd gone. I thought he could be taking them to our village to haggle over them, back of a pub, same one he was getting drunk in, swigging beer over his black mouth, spending Mum's money.

I heard it pule and looked up and saw the kite hovering over the clearing but it lunged away because I'd moved too quickly. Birds stayed if I kept very still. I waited but it didn't come back. I went down by the river and looked at the water. It was deeper here and it made no noise as it went by. It was smooth and shiny and when I looked just at the middle I couldn't tell if it was moving.

I realized there was nothing left to wait for and I knew I'd have to be like them now with today and tomorrow separate, bossing me. I'd have to lie and hide. And I'd always have to remember what he'd done to me, in the bathroom with the black still on him. And what he'd done to Mum.

I couldn't smell the river. The smell of the field didn't do anything. It was just another smell, not like his, the one I wanted to touch, keep by me, like I could with Rosko's, but I couldn't smell it when I tried to get it back, only the field. The yellowhammer started to sing and I heard Pockets doing Little-bit-of-bread-and-No-cheese, saying "cheese" funny, but I wanted to hate him too now, because he'd taken away what he could have given me if he wanted, because he knew. I wasn't sure if Rosko knew too; he probably did. I didn't want to hate. But I did. I threw a stone at the water and watched the circles get bigger and bigger and I threw another one in, making new circles cross some of the larger ones from before, but the flow soon moved them away. Like with Rosko, I thought, it was different with Pockets too, I couldn't hate him long. I would let him come back, and I began to then as I climbed up the bank, saying it was all right as long as he fetched the safe smell.

Her
Daughter

"We didn't get on. I never liked her. I didn't love her either. At first I tried to love her. Out of a sense of duty, I suppose. Because she was my mother. I know that's what made me say, once or twice, I loved her. When my sister Susan left home, she's two years younger than me, she told her straight she never liked her, called her a miserable old cow. She was always nasty to her so it was no surprise when she came out with that; Mother half expected it, I'm sure. This man, Vinny they called him, said he was taking Susan to Canada. He was quite a bit older than her. She was all over him. Couldn't see anything in him myself. He said he was going to make his fortune out there, said he'd give our Susan a much better life than she could even dream of in a hole like this. Can still see him standing there all pleased with himself after he said that. They met at a Saturday night dance. If there was a Saturday night dance somewhere Susan would find it. Mother told that Vinny she thought he was up to no good. He said Mrs. Thwaite this and Mrs. Thwaite that, like she was an imbecile or something. Fancied himself, did that one. 'Well, Mrs. Thwaite,' he said just before he went out the door, 'you can go please yourself, I don't give two farts what you think, she's coming with me and there's not a bugger you can do about it.' That was the last we saw of him. She told Susan he was a wideboy, said he'd drop her like a brick soon as the next skirt took his fancy. But it made no difference. Susan didn't give a damn what she said. Never had.

"It should get in on time. This one usually does. The late train's the worst. Truth is I'd rather not be going back. Anyway this is the last time I'll have to. . . . You know, with Susan everything was always in the open. Just the opposite from our mother. You knew where you stood with Susan. When she wanted something she'd shout and cuss till she got it. About three weeks after the do with him and Mother she left. We never heard from her again. Nothing. Not even a card to say she'd got there safe. She didn't care, did she. Still don't know where she is. Never knew if she went to Canada even. There's no way I can let her know about Mother dying. Not that she'd give a toss. That's Susan right through. She won't have changed any. I'd never have said the things she said to her, but I thought them plenty of times. Soon as I got this job in the city I left home. About a year after Susan went. Was a big relief to be out of there. For her too, I think, having me gone. She got on with the next-door neighbor all right but she pretty much kept herself to herself. We sort of stayed in touch. Same old obligation, I suppose. She never came to London. Once in a long while when I did go back I felt in the way. We had nothing to say to one another. We'd just sit there. Nothing ever changed. Same oilcloth on the kitchen table since I was a little kid. Almost worn away, hardly any red squares left on it. She never bought anything new if she could help it. Years of having to get by on nothing made her like that, I suppose. But she wasn't mean. I couldn't call her that. She could be mean sometimes, though. What she did have was kept spotless. The range sparkled. She blacked it once a week to keep it shining like that. She worked in a pottery painting colors on plates and vases and jugs and things. Went into that straight from school.

"Won't be any turkey this year. She always did a turkey. Her neighbor came over Christmas Day. She lives alone. She brought the pudding and some mince pies. Every time I said to myself, This is the last time I go. Talk about dreary. But I kept going. . . . When you're eating it you never think this could be your last, do you. Now the neighbor's asked me to stay on after the funeral, have Christmas with her, but I told her no. . . . This year seems to have flown by. Can't believe it'll soon be 1980. Doesn't seem five minutes since . . . She was only forty. Forty last June. I knew she was ill. Not that ill. Had no idea she was going to die that quick. The doctor said she had a . . . We're slowing down. Must be coming into the station. I'll get your case down now because I have to run to make sure of my bus. I'll leave it on the seat for you. It'll be easier for you to manage like that. This is it. Bye."

I rushed out into the corridor. I didn't want to hear her say anything soppy back. I knew she would. She had that kind of face. The compartment door sprung closed behind me. As I turned I saw her lips stop moving and I smiled at her through the glass. She smiled back. Smiling made her face look brittle. I lifted my hand to wave.

Nothing was appropriate. The man standing in front of me in the corridor was very large. When the train veered back after it pulled up it wedged him against his case, got him all jammed up. I was in a hurry. I tugged my bag round and made for the other door. I rushed past without looking in at her.

The bus wasn't there yet. I joined the people waiting. No one I recognized. Everyone was moving to try to keep warm. Some banged their feet, others rubbed their hands and one or two walked up and down slapping their sides. I thought about her being dead. Tried to picture what she'd be like: cold, pale, quiet, stiff, not so different from what she'd been alive, only now she had to be still, laid out with a sheet over. Some more joined the queue. They were lucky the bus was late, they said, and some of them who were waiting when I got there agreed they were lucky and said this was no weather to miss your bus in. One woman said it was no bloody weather to have to wait for one in either.

When it came thirty-five minutes after it was supposed to everyone scrambled on and most of us said, "About bloody time" as we did, some more than once. The conductor said there was no need to rush, there was plenty of room for this many and twice as many besides, but it made no difference we kept pushing and shoving to get to the seats. The bus dipped in and out of the potholes over the station forecourt with loud clonks. When the front wheel went into a deep one the bus lurched so steep it made the conductor run on the spot to get his balance back. He swore at the driver. Then he started this routine of stamping and shuffling his feet on the spot and he

managed to go backwards and forwards like that, keeping
his balance better. He whistled as he went.

"Any more fares now," he said. "Welcome to the rodeo."

"One to the Sitch, please," I said.

I held the money out but he missed because the bus
went down again and as it slewed the other way he skipped
back and took it and gave me my change with the ticket
sandwiched between the coins.

"Easy as she goes. Hold tight now."

He danced to the next fare.

The two in the seat behind me started on about immigrants coming in the country and taking jobs they don't
have a right to.

"Send 'em all back," one said.

"Right and all," the other said.

Someone behind them joined in and said what about
the thirties then when there was higher unemployment
than now, when there were no immigrants to speak of.

"You a bloody commie or something," one of them
said back.

The old man sitting opposite me was asleep. I watched
him breathe. It moved his coat up and down gently.
Someone walked by after ringing the bell for the next
stop and I began to stare at the mud and salt caked on
the outside of the window.

Where's Dad, Mum?

I don't know.

He never came home.

No.

Why?

He doesn't live here anymore.

Why?
I don't want him to.
I do.
I know but —
Does he still love me?
Yes.
Are you going away?
No, why would I.
Dad did.
Don't worry, we'll manage.
But I want him come back.
It'll be all right.

Him coming to get his things, telling her he wouldn't be coming back, not anymore he'd had enough. Him going out the door, slamming it so the house shook, after he stretched back in to snatch his best cap off the peg. I liked his hat. He put it on my head once. He hardly ever played with us. Me peeping from behind her, holding her legs. . . . Never saw him again. Susan said, "What dad?" one day when we were coming from school. (She couldn't remember him.) She knew she must have had one, she said, biology teacher said everybody had to, but who knows who he was except our mother and she won't tell anything; anyway who cares, not me, I'm here, aren't I. She laughed and then we both laughed at what she'd said. We got used to being without. "So what if you've got a dad," we'd say to the other kids when they asked, "we haven't, so there." Was like something out of a history lesson, too remote to have any feeling for: a date, a name in the past, a face you make up to go with it. It's important, the past, they kept telling us and I kept thinking, What for. All we wanted then was the end of the lesson, the bell to ring. Doesn't all fade. . . . You can remember if you try being snuggled in my arms, Susan, wrapped round me under the blankets, as we tried to hide from them going at each other downstairs, can't you. You heard them but you said, "I can't remember." . . . Shouting and hitting downstairs. . . . Sometimes I wish you'd come back, Susan, write or something. But where would you write now she's gone. You think I still live with her. If you ever think of me at all. Not known at this address it'd come back. Then you might guess she was dead. You know she'd never have moved. If you knew she was dead you wouldn't care, would you? Would you, Susan? I don't mind if you don't. Truth is I don't myself very much. Things are going very nicely for me at work right now. Buying my own flat. Managed to get a mortgage when I got my rise. We could get on if you came back, I'm sure. I'm not so bad as you think. I live in the big city now. It's stopping again. This bus takes forever. . . . They're burying her in the church graveyard next to Grandma Sapper. On the school side. She told Beth, you remember Beth her next-door neighbor, told her one evening when she was getting her washing in that she did not want to be cremated. Beth had been talking about her husband Harold's ashes, saying she wanted the same as what he had done, when her time was up. There's no will I know of. Why should there be. She can't have expected to die so soon. Phoned the local solicitor Malbrat to see if . . . He said he had no Hazel Thwaite as a client and he knew of no will being entrusted to him in that name. . . . There wasn't much time when the hospital called. I went straightaway. But it was too late. She was gone by the time I got there. They asked me did I want to see her anyway. No, I said. I didn't want to look at a corpse, especially hers. They told me that there was no more they could have done. Blast crisis, they said it was. They were going to do a postmortem on account of her age. They have to. So I got the next train back to London. We had to put the funeral off while they did that. She made pretty light of it when I asked her what was wrong with her, just said the treatment was working. It was Beth who let me know in the first place she was sick. I thought it was anemia or something. I don't think she knew what she had. Thought I should be feeling worse as I stood there in the hospital listening to them say how sorry they were, but I felt no loss. So I tried to make myself feel sad. Stupid, wasn't it. To keep up appearances. You wouldn't have done that, would you. Not our Susan. Postmortem. She's dead. Dead as a doorpost.

None of her father's side of the family will be there tomorrow. They never spoke to her after she refused to go to his funeral. Except Fay, but she never liked anyone on that side of the family. Besides she isn't blood and it's too far for her to come. There's only Ruth left on Mother's side. She's in a home. Completely cuckoo. Wait a minute. You won't know about Uncle Graham, Mother's brother. He was killed in a pit accident. Twenty-three miners died in the explosion. It was awful. Waiting at the pithead hoping, she said, along with all the other families, for your body to be pulled up alive. . . . Beth will be there if she can get the time off work. Sure I locked that cabinet before I left. I must have. Mrs. Rock.

I'm sure I did. The Shain file was on top. Mrs. Rock'll
be there. You know, the first person in the road to have
a phone and everyone wanted to try it but most of them
had no one to call. Ben Whitlock might be there. He
had a soft spot for Mother. He never got anywhere with
her. And Mrs. Reade from the post office who Beth says
hasn't missed a funeral at the church for sixty years. Not
much of a turnout, is it. You're well off out of it. Much
sooner not have to go myself. There was stuff at work I
wanted to get tied up before the holiday. . . . We were
never close. Never argued the way you two did but all
the same there was no love lost between us. The woman
I was talking to on the train never said where she was
going. Was a heavy case for her to be carrying. There'll
be the house to sort out. Nothing you'd want out of there,
I know. There are some things I put in a box before I
left from when we were little: school photos, your Girl
Guide sash, a doll, and that red velvet dress Grandma
made for you. It was the only dress you liked. You rubbed
dirt in the one with blue flowers on it Mother bought for
you. Was she right about Vinny? They always let you
down in the end, men do. Look at them on the seat in
front. She's putting her tongue in his mouth. He's doing
it back to her. They don't care who sees. Funny to think
of it; remember how I kissed that girl Sarah, in the house
down Follyfield Road, you were there, on the lips. I didn't
know it was a girl I'd kissed till the lights came on. I told
you in your ear it was good as kissing a boy. You said I
was mad.

"Were you wanted Sitch, weren't it?" the conductor
said.

He made me jump.

"Yes," I said.

"Next stop."

I grabbed my bag from the rack under the locker where the conductor kept his tickets and change rolls and stood by the door holding the rail. The driver braked hard again.

"Got a maniac this week," the conductor said. "Regular driver's on the panel. Mind how you go out there. Ice about."

I stood facing the front of the bus trying to find my pocketbook in my bag. Before I did the bus pulled away, grinding as the driver changed gear, taking all the light with it along the Sitch towards the terminus. I watched it get dimmer. About the same time it was passing Spratt the butcher's it was down to a twinkle. The kissers would soon be in the dark, I thought. The streetlights were out. One or two flickered at the dark but never came on. I turned, pretty much feeling my way, into Bolt's Lane. There was some light now from the chip shop window. It was an uncomfortable glare compared to the warm yellowy glow the bus took away. The zip on my bag was jammed and as I tried to free it I thought, I don't know why, it would be wrong to eat chips out of a newspaper with my mother being buried tomorrow. Then someone came out with some and the smell of them, and vinegar, went all round me and the newspaper began to steam in the cold. I had to have some.

The heat from the friers steamed up my glasses as soon as I opened the door. I was wiping them clear when this woman said:

"You're Hazel Thwaite's eldest."

"Yes," I said.

"Thought so. Were a bad thing that with your mother."

"Yes."

"S'pose you've come for funeral tomorrow."

"Yes."

"Were a bad thing happened."

"I know."

I put my glasses back on but still didn't recognize the woman. I knew I should have. There was something familiar about her.

"You's gone up in the world since I last seen you. That's been a time back."

"What do you —"

"Look at them clothes for a start. They never came from no jumble sale."

"They're only —"

"Sticks out a mile. S'pose the likes of us inner good enough for you no more. In a chip shop?"

"Listen, I —"

"I'll tell our Carol I've seen you. She'll be pleased to hear how a lady's getting on, I'm sure."

She went out, her chip packet stuffed under her coat. I knew soon as she said "Carol" who she was. Carol Blatt's mother. Carol was in the same class as me at junior school. Her mother had aged a lot. Her hair was thin and the skin on her face hung loose like a bloodhound's. She made everybody's business her own. She didn't care what she said. I thought as I looked over and through the glass at the pile of golden brown chips, She's probably jealous even when someone dies because of all the attention they're given.

Two miners in front of me were talking about whippets, about this man in Ball Green who had this whippet that had never lost a race, how it could come from nowhere and leave the rest for dead, how the man always sat up with it before a race, and how he always tasted the dog's food before the dog did. Now there was talk the dog had been nobbled but they didn't believe it; just trying to get the bugger's odds lengthened for the start of the season, they said. They hadn't noticed me but that bitch was still making me embarrassed. I thought of the things I should have said to her.

"Fish'll be up in a couple of ticks," Mr. Garr said.

He stood back from the frier, where he'd just flipped the fish over in the hot fat with a flat sieve on a long handle. The fat sizzled louder as he rolled them over. He wiped his hands down his apron and said to the miners:

"It's all lard, you know, none of that polyundersaturated stuff in there."

They paid no attention to him. They were arguing about overtime now. He turned to me. I knew he knew who I was.

"If you just want chips, luv, come on, these is waiting on fish."

I pressed up against the warm steel counter front and took some money from my pocketbook.

"Take no notice of her, her's a bad bugger," he said.

He gave the fish another prod with the thing. They spat at him.

"What can I do you for?"

"Small chips," I said.

"Sorry to hear about your mother."

"Yes."

"Her were never one for my chips, you know."

He grinned at me and I saw the black tooth you couldn't see when he was talking. I hadn't a clue what the hell he was talking about. We always got chips from him when we had any. Lots of times she fetched them. She always said they were good chips. I just wanted him to shut up and give me some.

"Happens to all of us sooner or later," he said. "When your number's on the ticket . . . Salt and vinegar?"

I nodded, and handed him a pound note, hoping he'd trip into his own fat and frizzle.

"That's all right, luv, keep it," he said. "I'm sorry to hear about your mother."

He pushed the money back at me and held out the newspapered chips for me to take. I had to thank him now.

Outside, looking back at the condensation run down his windows, I said out loud, "You can keep your bloody chips," and before the vinegar had soaked through the paper I hurled them over the wall into his back yard. I moved my bag to my right hand and walked away. It was beginning to feel heavy by the time I reached Hays Lane.

Mother's house was blacked out. I don't know what I expected. Upstairs or downstairs all the other houses in the row had some light coming from them, through a gap in the curtains or over the door. There was no one about. I climbed the five steps to the walkway. I could feel the hollows in them, worn like that by miners' boots. I stood outside the house, put my bag down, and looked up at the window of the room I used to sleep in. But then I didn't want to remember. I picked it up again and turned quickly into the entry. There was just enough light coming from Beth's scullery window to make my way by. I knocked at the door. She opened it and pushed her head out just past the lintel. She had a woolen hat on and a muffler. I looked behind me at Mother's door.

"She's not in there," she said. "Undertaker's got her."

"I know."

"Expected you a while back."

"I stopped for some chips."

I thought about his black tooth. I wasn't hungry so I said nothing about throwing them away because I knew she would only try to force some food down me if I did.

"You could have had something here," she said.

"I know, thanks, but the smell as I passed the chip shop."

"Come on in, chick."

She pulled the door open to let me pass, and closed it very gently as if she was trying not to wake someone. Perhaps this was a habit she got into when Harold was alive and working nights. He died when I was about five but she never stopped talking about him. I could see now she was dressed for outdoors with a heavy brown coat, and boots.

"Just come in?" I said.

"No. I was waiting for you. I want you to come with me."

"Where?"

"I waited for you so we could go together."

"Go where?"

She was nervous, twitchy almost. I wondered if I was acting strange. She was, poking her head out at me like that as if I was a stranger she had to give the once-over to. We were both uneasy. All the years in and out of one another's houses suddenly seemed to count for nothing.

"I know it sounds daft," she said. "But I want you to come up Holdworth's farm with me."

"What? Now?"

"Yes."

"Up by the hill? That Holdworth's?"

"Yes."

"What for? It's freezing out there."

"I can't explain, believe me. Just come."

She opened the door of the range and told me to sit in front of it. The coals were red. She stood back away from the heat. She was impatient.

"Won't take you a minute to get warm in front of that. I've put something in Harold's old flask for after."

I was annoyed with her for being so cagey. I turned, looked across at her and stared, puzzling. I was going to say something but she spoke first.

"I was the last one to see her. Was quick after they fetched her to the hospital."

"By the time I got there it was too . . . It was good someone close was with her."

Better Beth than me, I thought.

"I would have phoned you myself but that doctor I met told me it would be better if he contacted the family so I —"

"You did everything you could getting the ambulance here, then going to be with her."

She turned her head and lifted it. The light that way touched the side of her face, softening it. It was hard to believe just then she was eleven years older than Mother.

"That fetched them out their houses when the ambulance came clanging," she said. "They gawked and mumbled all the time they were getting her stretcher into the ambulance. I'm sure she could hear what they were saying about her."

"The doctor told me she had no pain at the end."

"She looked peaceful when I saw her. I was down there in plenty of time. Soon as the doctors finished with her they let me in to see her. Told them I was a relative, her sister, in fact."

She swallowed.

"She made, made . . ."

She stopped then started again.

"She made me promise. Wasn't sure I should tell you. Don't know what to think. . . . You might as well know. Can't see what harm it can do now. She knew I'd do what she wanted me to, didn't she. But she still made me promise, before she told me what it was. . . . Said she wanted me to go up by Holdworth's farm after dark and watch the pit. I asked her what for but she said nothing else. She was slipping fast. Truth is I don't want to go up there by myself but I promised her. On her deathbed I . . . Should have gone the night she died but I waited 'cause I thought you'd go with me when you came. I knew you'd come."

I didn't tell her what I was thinking. Just said I'd go. Seemed the easiest thing to do.

We walked quickly. There were a few clouds scudding

by but it was mostly clear, with a small moon and plenty of stars. Halfway up Nipps Bank we had a struggle because the road was covered with a sheet of ice for quite a way. We held on to each other, shuffling up it, the moon always one step ahead of us. We slipped back a few times, and on the steepest part Beth began to slide; she grabbed me tighter so both of us went down. We must have looked like a couple of clowns as we tried to stand up, but once we were on our feet we made it to the end of the ice without falling. At the top of Nipps Bank the tall hedge-rows give way to stone walls and for the first time we could see over into the fields, where the road turns sharply and levels out. She took out the flask and gave it to me. The whisky burned my throat but it was warming. She took it from me, tipped it back and gulped. When we got to the gate at the top of the track that led down to Holdworth's farm she took it out again and began to swig freely but she didn't offer me any this time.

I looked behind me. Just the smooth rounded outline of the hill above us was all I could see. When I turned she lifted the flask to her mouth one more time and finished it off. We leaned against the gate. There was no wind. Below in the dip we could pick out the tops of the roofs of the farm buildings and the tops of the end walls because their edges were darker than the night. There was a feather of smoke from one of the chimneys. Way beyond across the other side of the hollow, directly be-hind the farm, in and out of the colliery yard, we could hear the headstocks from the coal trains screak and clank over the tracks, and jangle, and we could see steam off the pump engines rise up between the conical slag heaps

and vanish before it passed their tops. And deep underneath, in the pother, were men, from families we knew,
covered in coal dust.

"What now?" she said.

"Don't know. Think you've kept your promise?"

"I've watched it, haven't I. I came up here."

"She said nothing else?"

"It's all she asked me to do."

"Nothing more?"

"No."

"You sure?"

" 'Course I am. . . . She did mumble something right
at the end but you couldn't make it out."

"None of it?"

"Nothing."

"That's it then."

"What?"

"We're wasting our time."

"What d'you mean?"

"Standing here freezing. We're never going to find out
why."

"I had to come."

"I'm not saying you didn't. Just there's no point staying
any longer, is there."

"What do you think she was getting after then?"

"I said I don't know. Probably confused with the drugs
they had her on."

"I've made a fool of myself, that's what you're thinking,
isn't it."

"You did what you said you would, didn't you. Let's
go back."

She took out the flask again. Shook it.

"Empty. It's bloody empty."

"We'd better take the top road to miss that ice."

"Some in the house. Not to worry."

After a few steps she turned to look back. She hoped to find something, I'm sure, because all the way home she kept on looking behind her as if she believed the dark had the answer and was spitefully keeping it from her. By the time we got back it was clouded over and looked like it was going to snow.

She went into the house first and told me to lock the door and pull the curtain across it. She was on her knees when I looked, pulling soap powder boxes and cleaning liquids from the cupboard under the sink.

"Here it is, I knew there was one somewhere," she said. "Thank Christ."

She stood up, one hand on the bottom of her back, placed a full bottle of Bells on the draining board, then unbuttoned her coat without taking her eyes off the whisky.

"I just want to forget about that out there," she said. "It's spooky."

She kicked her boots off. One of them knocked over a packet of Daz. She left it there spilling out. Only the bottle concerned her.

"Drugs, you said. You could be right. Anyway let's have a drop of this before we turn in."

She unscrewed the cap urgently but she wasn't clumsy with it. She poured some and handed me a tumbler with quite a lot in.

"This'll warm us up," she said. "I'll make the fire up. I try to keep it in this time of year. With the price of coal you . . . That feels better. We'll have time to talk after tomorrow's over. You go on up, chick. Best be fresh for the morning. I'll not be long after."

She'd put me in the little room at the back. The single bed took up most of it. They looked like urns on the wallpaper. It was hard to tell, the print had faded so much. I slept lightly. I woke about six, the day racing ahead of me for the worst, like it often does when you don't want to do something. I heard Beth underneath, pottering in the kitchen, and thought I could smell whisky. She turned the radio on; it was news but I couldn't quite make out what they were saying. I wasn't interested anyway. Same old stuff. Fighting and disasters. When I sat up I saw Mother's patch of garden through the piece of old lace covering the bottom half of the window. It was a tangle of frozen weeds. It had been a picture when I saw it last summer: red and white hollyhocks against the fence with lupins and irises gently moving their colors in front of them, and blue lobelia, and nasturtiums pushing orange everywhere, and antirrhinums and alyssum dotted around with marigolds, and in the center, with a bed to themselves, roses were opening their first flush. Yes. She was different when she was doing her garden.

The lino was so cold when I stood on it I jumped back on the bed and got dressed. I began to feel it stronger, not wanting to be there, let alone having to go to her funeral two days before Christmas and put on a miserable face. There was nothing in it for me. I knew she had no money to leave and there was nothing in her rented house worth more than a tinker's curse. But as I watched my breath condense over the bed I began to wonder about it. The way she had skimped got me to thinking there had to be something left somewhere; and with her not making any will I knew of, whatever it amounted to would be mine, all of it, as long as they couldn't find Susan. I wouldn't be able to help them with that because I hadn't a clue where she was. She could be dead as well for all I knew.

I finished dressing and went downstairs. Inheriting the money was still very much on my mind as I walked in the kitchen.

"Cup of tea?" she said.

"Please."

"Sleep all right?"

"Yes, thanks."

"Don't matter what time I get to sleep, I wake at five. Regular as clockwork. Still doing shifts, aren't I."

She laughed at what she said. It made her cough. She was still coughing when she bent down to open the oven.

"Here, I've done you some oatcakes and bacon."

It was whisky I could smell.

"You remembered I liked oatcakes."

"Doesn't take much remembering."

The bacon was crisp, how I like it. She spooned me some fried tomatoes over the oatcakes and put a dollop of bubble by the bacon.

"Aren't you having some?" I said.

"I never eat breakfast nowadays but it's nice to have someone to get it for."

She looked thin even with a heavy jumper on. I thought, She can't be eating much anytime. She put the fry pan

in the sink and reached behind the plates standing in the
rack on the draining board to pick something up. It was
a tumbler half full of Scotch. She came to the table with
it, sat down with it. I'd smelled right.

"Did my mother leave anything with you?" I said.

"No, nothing. Were you expecting . . ."

"No. I was just wondering. These oatcakes. Mmm."

"Have some more."

"No, thanks, I'm all right. But I'd love another cup of
tea."

"There you are. Put your own milk in. You know how
much you like."

"What time they picking us up? They really are deli-
cious."

"Been making 'em long enough, they ought to be.
Quarter to two, they said."

"That gives us plenty of time."

"Bubble were Harold's favorite. It's only leftovers but
he loved it."

"What's the weather supposed to do?"

"Not going above freezing all day, they said. Windy.
Should stay fine."

She sipped her whisky keeping both hands round the
glass.

"Funny having you in the house again. Remember
when you —"

She stopped, got up jerkily and went to the range to
put some coal on. I thought I knew what she was going
to say, why she hadn't finished. I didn't press it. Not
then. We had a funeral to get through. As I watched her
rake the grate I started to feel resentful.

I put on my coat while she was doing the dishes and walked down to the florist's shop to pay for the wreaths that Beth had ordered. She told them what she wanted written on hers. I had to give them something to write on my label and be quick about it. They had to be delivered to the undertaker's. How do you send a wreath and not send it sincerely, I thought. But lots of people must; what about all the ambulance chasers. I bet half the messages written on those things aren't meant. It's easy to write what you want. Who'll know. Besides everyone goes along with it. Nobody'll call you a liar at a funeral. I scribbled, "Your loving daughter Hazel," then crossed it out and wrote, "Your daughter Hazel," and gave it to the woman who was standing there waiting with her hands on her apron. As I walked out the shop, smelling the hyacinths all the way, I hoped it would rain or snow so that even the truth would be washed off the card before anyone could read it. After the funeral there was no way of knowing what people might say.

Beth was standing in front of Mother's when I got back, ready to leave, with her hat pinned in place and her fifties navy blue coat pulled up at the collar. She looked lost in it.

"I closed the curtains the day she died," she said.

I hadn't noticed before. The faded maroon curtains were pulled tight across the downstairs window. She seemed pleased with herself for doing it.

"I'd forgotten you had to do that," I said. "Why you ready so soon? There's no hurry."

"Finished clearing up. Had nothing to do. Not used to having time on my hands."

"But out here? It's freezing."

"Wanted to get out the house for a bit."

"One forty-five, you said?"

"Yes."

"I'm going in."

"We ought be outside when the coffin comes. It's only proper."

"We will."

I had a black coat and a pair of gloves to match but no hat. I wasn't going to wear one. I dislike hats but she said I ought to wear something over my head, out of respect. She found me a scarf. I put it on to keep the peace.

We were waiting outside when the hearse pulled up. Our wreaths were on top of the coffin. There were two others beside them and some flowers, which lay touching the window. I wondered who they were from, what they said. The polished black car we were riding in pulled up seconds later. The door was opened for us exactly at the bottom of the steps by a tall, skinny man. He didn't look at us or say anything. He was trying not to be noticed. He wasn't very good at it. He could keep very still but the way he bent over made you very aware of him because he looked as if he was about to topple on you. Across the road in a line, standing against the wall, were six or seven miners from the terrace, with their caps in their hands. One, Mr. Tinkley (I remember him chasing us as kids when we taunted him over his big red conk), had his Jack Russell sitting next to him. The dog looked wistfully up at him as it shivered but it was too afraid to move. Having come off nights the miners would usually be in bed at this time but a funeral was a special occasion in the road. Most of the women who were home would be peeping from inside their houses. Only Beth's next-door neighbor on the other side (a new woman I didn't know) and Mrs. Field stood outside. The milkman had stopped his float near the end of the terrace and was leaning against it with two pints in his hand, also looking on. "It's a shame," I heard the new woman say as we went down the steps. "Yeah," Mrs. Field said back, "she was a sad one, was her." He closed the door. The people in the road would be joined by others after we'd gone, mostly women. They'd come out to help make the most of a death in the road. They'd all prattle away and the old hands would come up with fresh stories to make sure it was a memorable day. No one could be sure when their next chance would be.

As the hearse pulled away I saw the men cross to the other side of the road so they could see it round the first bend. The dog began to yap at being able to move again. It jumped up after the cap one of the miners was holding and missed but tried again, this time to meet the knuckles of his closed fist hard on its muzzle. Death doesn't mean much to a dog, I thought, not as much as jumping after a cap anyway. I was on the dog's side. Beth looked even more lost in her coat now that she was sat down in the corner of the large leather seat because the loose fabric was pushed up, and bagged around her. Her head was bowed, her chin hidden by the collar. I watched the coffin weave gently in front of us, never getting any nearer to it, never getting further away, until we reached the churchyard.

They unloaded the coffin onto a polished chrome trolley. When they were ready to push it up the path that wound between the graves to the church porch, the same tall man walked over to open the door for us but this time did it more deliberately, as if he'd given up on his act. We stood in the blustering wind. Beth looked pale as she held on to her hat, loose strands of hair blowing behind, gray. The undertaker asked us to wait behind the coffin. He took Beth by the arm. We waited there until the vicar came with his prayer book, down the hill, to lead the procession.

We walked in silence. When the ground began to level out the pallbearers lifted the coffin from the trolley and carried it. A short distance from the church the vicar started in his doleful voice:

"I am the resurrection and the life saith the Lord."

I kept my eyes on the coffin. It listed as it was moved along, because the pallbearers, being different heights, were unable to keep it level when they took fresh steps. As the wreaths slid towards his corner the shortest bearer had to knock them back while taking all the weight on one arm; he couldn't see too well over his shoulder so once or twice he jabbed at the side of the coffin with his fist. We could all hear it resound, but the vicar kept going.

"Though she were dead yet shall she live. . . ."

She is dead, I said to myself. Behind you. See for yourself. Dead. Dead. Dead.

"After my skin worms. . . ."

The wind whistled round his words.

When we reached the porch we all had to wait again while they placed the coffin back on the trolley and rear-ranged the flowers. Beth and I were told to follow as it was wheeled up the aisle behind the vicar, and when we reached the front to sit in the pew on the right. Halfway up the aisle I noticed some people but I didn't turn to see who they were. Because I didn't want to pay for an organist we had to say Psalm 39, which the vicar seemed to delight in announcing. We said it, in a perfunctory sort of way, him louder than anyone else, one flat word after another. I'm not sure why but when we got to the bit, maybe because I wasn't sure what it meant, about a moth fretting a garment I stopped reading and just re-peated under my breath "a moth fretting a garment," until the rest reached the end of the psalm and said "Amen," the vicar saying "Amen" longer than anyone else, making a meal of it. He read more about the dead being raised and then we walked slowly to the grave. Mother was carried in front of us.

All I saw was his cassock flap flap flap in the wind until they lowered the coffin into the hole, and then I just stared at it lying there at an angle over a rock, a polished box stranded.

He started to speak again but the wind carried most of his words the other way. I preferred the wind, with his mouth open, just the wind coming out. The pallbearer who had banged against the coffin seemed to know when to come over from the path. He gave me a handful of gritty soil and said into my ear to throw it into the grave. It was frozen. The coffin sounded like a snare drum when it hit it. The vicar made the sign of the cross in the air with two pointed fingers and I heard Beth crying then. I looked at the ground.

Afterwards I stood by myself over the grave. I didn't bother to see who the flowers were from. The wind had got up even stronger. I was thinking about bodies decomposing when the sexton came along. He thrust his shovel into the mound of soil piled up at the other side; part of it gave way and slid into the grave and broke into pieces on the coffin lid. Once the mound was settled he leaned on his shovel, waiting for me to go so he could fill it in. I tried to remember what she looked like but I couldn't form a picture, yet I knew if I got down in there and prized it open I'd recognize her in a flash. I looked at the sexton instead. He was struggling to light a cigarette. I stepped back on the path where I saw the vicar coming towards me. He had to shout when he reached me to make me hear something about it was God's wish, how I must try not to forget that, how God had given us everything so it was his to take away when he saw fit because his was the ultimate wisdom and so long as we knew that and trusted in it there was nothing to worry about I would see my mother again. How could I tell him I didn't want to. He held my arm and began walking me down the path. We were nearly at the gate when he let go. He smiled. I knew we had to pay him something for the service but I thought the undertaker was supposed to take care of it. I nodded. He smiled again and walked back up the hill. Beth sat in the same corner of the limousine subdued, tearful, but the red the wind had put on her cheeks made her look comical. I looked out of the rear window. He'll have her well covered with soil and cigarette butts by now, I thought as we rounded the corner and I lost sight of the graveyard.

Beth had asked Mrs. Rock back. She was waiting at the top of the steps when we got there, holding her bag across her middle with both hands. She said Ben Whitlock had wanted to attend the funeral but wasn't able to on account of his shingles. Beth said she saw Mrs. Reade at the back of the church. Mrs. Rock said she'd spoken to her afterwards and Mrs. Reade complained there was no hymn. She said she always liked a hymn at funerals especially when it was "Bread of Heaven." The people I noticed on the way in were from the pottery. Beth said she'd worked there long enough to be represented. Mrs. Rock said there was a wreath from Fay, whom she'd met some years before when she'd gone over to use her phone, and who she thought was a very nice woman. We drank tea from Beth's best cups and ate some biscuits and none of us knew what to say once Mrs. Rock finished talking about the funeral. I kept quiet but Mrs. Rock and Beth prevented a silence by telling each other they thought Hazel Thwaite, my mother, was a good woman, how there was never any way of knowing what was going to happen in life, and they ought to know, they said, because both their husbands had died in the prime of it. They went on, each trying to show she had suffered a greater loss than the other when her husband died. Beth talked of losing her husband, Mrs. Rock of having hers taken. They would have been at it even longer if Mrs. Rock hadn't remembered she had to get something before the shops closed. On her way out she said again she thought Hazel Thwaite was a good woman, and added, "It were a great pity."

We carried the dirty plates and cups through to the kitchen. Beth said the last time she used her front room was after Harold's funeral. There was still light outside but she turned the lamp on and pulled the curtain across. She took her cardigan off, put on an apron, and rolled up the sleeves of her dress before filling the bowl in the sink with hot water and squirting the Fairy liquid over it. She washed and I dried. She said nothing as she took extra care with her best china, lowering each piece onto the drainer with both hands. When she'd finished she dried her hands rubbing them over and over while she stared at the floor. Then with a jolt she said:

"That needs doing."

She wedged the end of the towel in the draw, left it dangling, and went over to stoke the fire. She poked until it all glowed red before putting more coal on.

"That should do it for a while," she said.

She put the coal scuttle back in the corner and went over to the dresser and grabbed the Scotch bottle by the neck.

"Reckon I need one," she said.

She wasn't subdued now. She poured some into a tumbler and took a gulp before placing the china onto a tray and taking it back into the front room. I sat down. I could hear the china clink against the glass as she put it back into the cabinet. She went straight for her tumbler when she came back and drank some before she put the tray away. I was edgy. I didn't want to keep it in any longer but at the same time I was trying not to blurt and make a fool of myself. I let it out.

"Do you think," I said. "Do you think I should have cared more?"

"What about?"

"My mother."

"What you getting at?"

She knew as soon as I asked. I was determined to make her answer. She poured more into hers, and this time got some for me. She handed me the Scotch and sat down with her apron on, her tumbler filled much higher than mine.

"I'm not getting at anything," I said. "You can't pretend after all this time that you don't know."

"It's no time to be talking about her like —"

"Why not?"

"Right after her funeral's why not."

"What's so wrong? You're not letting her down if that's what you think."

"It's not that."

"What then?"

"I don't know."

"It's because for as long as I can remember you've treated me as your own daughter, isn't it?"

"That's not why."

"You don't have a why. You trying to tell me you've never ever thought about it."

"No."

"I know you have. As well as you do."

"But I feel I owe it to her."

"Owe what, she's dead now."

"You don't understand."

"Don't I."

"No, you don't."

"You never said anything that might have made me think of changing my feelings about her because you liked it the way it was, making out I was yours. It suited you having me against her."

"You're cruel."

I didn't give a damn now what she thought.

"What's got into you?" she said.

"Nothing. Why must something have got into me because I asked a question."

She swigged more Scotch. Most of it. She was drinking heavily now. I knew she liked to take a drink but not that it had got this bad. She wiped her hand across her mouth and as she pursed her lips I thought, I want to blame you, smash your stupid illusion. I hadn't wanted to do that before.

"Won't be much of a Christmas, will it," she said. "Not now. Sure you won't stay?"

I shook my head. She stood up, got some more whisky, and sat down. I still had some in my tumbler.

"No," she said. "But I can't say I look forward to it in the first place. All money now is all Christmas is. For kids, if I . . . Your mother . . . She . . . You know you never treated her right."

She looked hard at the fire. I wanted more out of her now. I was about to goad her again when she said:

"I always wanted a baby. Harold couldn't."

She looked back at the fire. If I was going to I might have felt a bit sorry for her then. No. The silence was

fine. It held most of the power I needed. The booze held
the rest. She looked up and weakly turned towards me.

"I wanted my own child," she said. "More than anything I wanted a child. Have it grow inside me, get big
with it like other women I watched waddle around. I
went on trying to get pregnant and convinced Harold it
would be all right, long after they told us it was impos-
sible. Didn't have a live sperm in him, they said. They
had a fancy word for it. I made him believe it only needed
one, that he had to have one, what did doctors know.
But every month I got my period regular as clockwork.
I started thinking I could do it on my own with some
quack remedy so I did all kinds of things to myself. I went
half round the bend. I prayed. Don't think I didn't think
of going with another man. I felt more and more a freak.
Then I convinced myself I was swelling up and I would
feel the baby inside me and give it names, sometimes
girls' names, sometimes boys'. I bought bigger clothes
and put them on. I knew he felt less a man because he
couldn't do it. He blamed himself. For other women
around it seemed so easy. First time, they said. Only had
to pull his trousers down. Bull's eye. Bun in the oven.
You don't want to leave it too long, you know. Gets
harder the older you are. Sarah's in the club again and
Maud from work just had twins. Harold began to take
on more and more overtime, spend more time on his
allotment, work more round the house, to try make up
for it. I think he felt everything he was had been taken
from him when they told him his were no good. I told
him there was more in life than that but I didn't believe
it for one minute. No. Felt like a leper the way other

people looked at me. They knew there was nothing there. It was just a sham. And all I needed from him was one ripe seed. The one thing he never had. I didn't even care about the money he fetched home from the pit is how desperate I was. Just one tiny seed was all it would have taken. I was regular as clockwork. Fertile, they said. It weren't my fault.

"One night at the end of a heavy week he sat in his chair exhausted. Same chair you're in. He asked me to fetch him some beer. It was a warm evening. I went down the off-sales at the pub to get him some mild. The usual girl wasn't there. Jim Goran, the landlord, came over and asked me what I wanted. He smiled after he said what a nice evening it was. I only knew him to say hello to. I'd been in the lounge bar once or twice of a Saturday night with Harold when they had music, that's all. He said he'd have to get some pint bottles up from the cellar, he wouldn't be a minute. While he was gone I unbuttoned my blouse and unhooked my bra. He came back, put the bottles on the counter and went to get my change. As he came back I showed him, pulled my blouse open wide and stuck my tits out so he had to see. He put the change down trying not to look at them and walked away. I stood there stroking them for a minute or two but he stayed the other end of the bar. Never said a word to me. I never told no one but I know he did. Soon as I went out, I bet. Everyone in the village must have known next day. Except Harold. I didn't care. All I could think about was the baby. . . . Thought about stealing one. The doctor gave me some pills. Made me feel drowsy. They blurred things. I was beginning to get over it some when

your mother moved in next door but seeing her six months
pregnant with you brought it all back. She couldn't have
been long left school. She looked afraid. I never spoke
to her. Went out of my way to avoid her. If she was in
the yard I stayed indoors. I'm ashamed of it now but more
than once I hoped she'd lose the baby. . . . When you
were born it changed somehow. I don't know what it was
but I didn't feel that way anymore. I didn't stop wanting
the baby but the jealousy was gone. A few days after she
brought you home with her from the hospital I went over
and asked her if I could help any. She seemed happy to
let me and told me you were called Hazel like she was.
I think she'd been too worried with it all before to notice
I'd kept out of her way. Anyway she never said anything
about it. It made me feel better being around you, changing you and rocking you to sleep after I'd done your bottle.
Never seemed to bother her none me taking you away
from her."

She looked into her glass and rolled the drop that was
left round and round. This time the silence didn't press
her so I did.

"You think that's what started it then?"

"What?"

"Me not liking her."

She stood up but stayed by her chair.

"How should I know."

"You ought to."

"Why? . . . I did nothing wrong. Why should I blame
myself when I did nothing wrong."

"So you don't mind blaming me or her, is that it."

"I never said that."

"You didn't have to."

She moved the bottle. The top was off from the last time. She gave herself more and without letting go of the bottle leaned over with it, knocking the neck against the rim of my tumbler. The whisky gurgled out. I had to push the tumbler up forcefully to stop it coming because she was balancing on it.

"Why are you carrying on with this?" she said.

Without answering I looked at the fire and waited.

"Please yourself. I've seen it all before," she said.

She put the bottle down with a thump. What whisky was left in it jumped up the sides and fell back without splashing out the top. She turned towards the fire and before flopping back into her chair she made a spluttering noise with her lips. She spilled whisky on herself as she went down.

"Why do you do this," she said. "After all I've done . . ."

She stopped, took a mouthful, swilled it over her teeth a few times before gulping it back, then started again but not where she left off. I told myself, Let her go on, don't say anything to her now.

"I don't care what you think. . . . I don't. You can please yourself, I mean it. Why should I gi — He was a drinker, you know, your father. Don't go getting no ideas about me because. . . . Was no secret around here was that. Many a night he came stumbling up that alley out there pissed as a parrot with his pockets pulled inside out swearing at your mother because all the money was gone. And you ask me if I started it. You don't know the half."

A piece of coal near the top of the fire whispered, blew

puffs of green smoke between the bars, then hissed and started to flame. She watched. The coal stopped hissing and began to sputter a dull sound, a sort of popping. She continued watching. As the sputtering got faster the flames reached higher, and seemed to absorb her more. I was wrong about thinking she would go on talking without being prompted, because the booze suddenly had her another way when I'd only counted on it making her talk; now it was pushing her into herself, depressing her. After a few minutes I badgered, trying to get her to open up again, but she ignored me, held her eyes resolutely on the flickering coal and gripped her hands tight around the tumbler. I wanted to let go altogether, let her have it straight out, no messing, but I tried the other approach.

"Beth, I'm sorry," I said. "I really would like to know what happened back then. You know Mother wouldn't say anything to me, or Susan. I didn't mean to be nasty. I shouldn't have. It's been a difficult day for both of us, I know it has. I'm sorry."

My dissemblance worked. I wasn't sure it would with her acting so fickle and that baby plying her mind. This was the first I knew about the difficulties wanting a baby had caused her. I'd always imagined, I suppose, that they'd adjusted well to not being able to have kids. I'd always heard her speak fondly of Harold till now. Still I don't ever remember them fighting.

She loosened her grip on the glass. When she turned towards me her look was softened.

"You won't remember Harold," she said.

"He gave me jelly babies," I said.

As soon as I said it I realized. It was unintentional. He

did give me jelly babies. That's all I meant. I wasn't trying to hurt her. Either she didn't make the connection, which is unlikely, or she was giving me the benefit of her doubt.

"Not well, I mean," she said. "You won't remember him well. You were too young to when he died."

Christ knows why I ever had to let her mother me, I thought. She was always a wreck if I'd known.

"He never drank like your father, did Harold," she said. "Never saw him drunk once all the time we were married. A pint or two of mild was all he took. Wasn't only the drink. I thought it was. All the time he was living there I thought it was the drinking was the cause of the trouble. She never said otherwise. No. Then she didn't talk to me much above passing the time of day and telling me what had to be done with you. That's how it was till your sister was born. She seemed afraid almost of being friendly. When Susan came she pretty much cut off what bit of contact we did have saying she could manage all right without my help when it was bloody obvious she had twice as much work on her hands than before. So for a long while there were even fewer words passed. I couldn't make it out. Harold said it was him, Tom, your father, he must have told her not to have any more to do with me. Must have had one of his moods on him, Harold said, and told her I was interfering or something. 'When doesn't the bugger have one on him,' I said. Mind you, your mother could be funny at times for no reason at all. I don't know what it was caused it. Maybe Harold had it right. I never figured out it was anything I said had given offense. I worried. You do. You say to yourself you don't care but you do, don't you.

You know with all she had on her hands she only let me
do some ironing once in a while to help out. Only when
she was really pushed. All them baby clothes on top of
his black shirts from the mine. She would bring it over
all secretive like, try to leave it on the table there as if
this pile of laundry the size of a house was invisible.
Pretending, I don't doubt, she wasn't really asking me.
She kept that acting-distant stuff up. Wouldn't stay for a
cup of tea even. What peeved me most was I couldn't
see you. That had to be him, mean Tom Thwaite, not
letting her bring you over, threatening her. When you
were out playing in the garden I'd go talk to you through
the fence. If he was there she'd come out and fetch you
in soon as she saw me. She knew how much pleasure
you gave me even if she never knew all of why. I never
let on to her about how badly I wanted my own kid. I'd
learned to keep it to myself more by the time she moved
in. She had a canny way with her. She could have known.
Stories in this place die slowly if they ever do. Things
get pieced together from scraps. Never thought of it before. No. But if she'd found out about what I did in the
pub that time she might have kept you from me because
of it. . . . He carried on no different, your father. Just
the same as when you were born. Pit and pub. Only thing
he ever lifted around the house was his fist. With him
you never knew. He'd never settle. It was like something
was chasing after him all the time. From what we heard
he was no different in the pub. Harold said he was the
same at work, surly-like, always on the move. Harold
tried to be friendly to him being neighbors and all, but
what was the use. It seemed to make him worse when

you tried to have anything to do with him. No, she wouldn't let me see you after Susan came.

"Never forget how he made me jump. One Monday morning I was hanging the washing out. Suddenly noticed him from the corner of my eye. Scared the wits out of me. Don't know how long he'd been watching. He'd never stopped even to say hello before, and here he is all of a sudden staring at me. Something was up. Him standing there, in his good clothes, with his hands in his pockets, slouching with his cap well back on his head. When I looked at him proper I knew all right. He was eyeing me dirty and soon as he'd caught my eyes he started grinning at me dirty too. I carried on with my pegging but I could feel him still doing it. He wasn't drunk. I knew that much. There was none of that in his eyes. I bent down to get some more washing from the basket. He said, 'That's all a woman is, is a washing machine with tits.' Knew better than say anything back for fear of getting it worse for her, he'd be bound to take it out on her if I had a go at him. He walked into the house. I looked at his broad back and his curly black hair sticking out under his cap and for a second forgot what he'd said and wondered should I let him, it'd be a pretty baby like you. He slammed the door after him. I flushed hot with the shame of it. I wanted to kill him. But I thought it again and again after that. It sort of fixed on my mind that he could give me the baby, that it'd never turn out bad like him because he wouldn't come near it, never know it was his in the first place. All the week after when Harold was on nights I lay in bed for hours imagining Tom Thwaite come up our stairs to take what his dirty eyes had asked for and me pulling up my nightie in the dark to let him, not caring because the baby would be mine, not his. I planned to tell Harold it was his, that I was right, he did have one good one in him, he should have believed me.

"Not long after the day he stood there with his lecher eyes on me he was gone. I'd heard your mother and him fighting just before. But I expected him to roll up the entry drunk, sooner or later, rows were nothing new, with his foul mouth echoing ahead of him. He never came. Weeks went by. She never told me he'd left. She didn't have to, I know, I could see for myself, but you'd have thought she'd say something if only to make it easier for her. But no. That's how she was. . . . She came round slowly. . . . She started back at the pottery, same place she worked right up to the time you were born. I wasn't working then so I minded you in the day. You were good as gold. Your gran took Susan. She was still charring, your gran was, so she had her hands full as well. I was happy getting you back, having you to myself. From then on I pretty much took care of you until . . . I don't see nothing wrong with that. Did you no harm . . . Your mother never heard from him again as far as I know. No money or anything ever came. Not that she expected it. She weren't that stupid. Harold said it was funny him not showing up for work the day he left because the pit held a week's wages in hand. Far as I know money's still waiting for him. There were rumors. There always are. Truth's never enough on its own, is it. It went round he'd moved in with a woman in Burslem he'd been seeing on the side. Then they said he'd gone to Nottingham where he had cousins and got a job in a pit there. Some-one said they'd seen him working in a pub in Blackpool as a pot man. I didn't give a monkey's where he'd gone. I weren't the only one, I knew that. Good riddance is what a lot round here thought. Nor was she sorry, your mother. She wanted him out of there, I know she did. . . . There's another bottle around here somewhere. I'll find it."

She was a little unsteady on her feet when she got out of the chair. She looked in the dresser. It wasn't there. It wasn't under the sink where she got the last one from. She went into the other room determined but came back empty-handed. Under a housecoat on the peg on the back of the door hung a shopping bag. She found it in that. She tossed the empty bottle in the ash bucket, banged the full one down in its place, and as the dust was settling timidly over the hearth and some over the rug, she man-aged after a few goes to unscrew the cap. She poured herself some Scotch and took a drink.

"Do you think we have choices," she said. "We don't have any bloody choice."

She turned away from the bottle, looked at the fire. I didn't say anything. She threw some coal on. Some pieces missed. They scattered the dust further as they bounced across the tiles. She left them there. This time she had difficulty sitting down. She began to let herself go, then as if she felt she was going to fall she stiffened and stood up straight. She got down the second go. Once she was settled she picked up the whisky without spilling any. The wind rattled the door. She didn't notice; she was bent over holding her comfort and gazing at the blue smoke rise off the fresh coal. I knew I shouldn't say anything. The wind came again. I stared at the door, thought of her buried out there, how dark in the ground, that it was her, featureful, who Beth was talking about, alive, not yet some faceless remains her name wouldn't fit anymore. But alive or dead brought her no nearer to me. I think curiosity just then, more than anything, made me want her to carry on telling it. I looked at the bottle then at the clock on the dresser. It had stopped. What difference did it make, I thought as I turned and saw her slumped in the chair. Her eyes were closed. I moved up in my chair. It disturbed her, and when she looked across she seemed surprised to find me there. She started talking again without realizing, I think, she had drifted off.

"I like the smell of the blue smoke," she said. "Something about it. . . . Could have been the same day he died but I can't be sure. Anyway it had to be soon after."

"Same day who died?" I said.

"Her father. Linden Sapper. She came over special that evening to tell me he'd finally suffocated. I might have guessed something when she said 'finally.' . . . She wasn't sad like you'd expect. Was a look on her I'd not seen before. Sort of satisfied look. . . . Soon as she was in the door she said she was glad he was dead. Said her mother was too, only her mother was afraid to say it, now that what she had been waiting for so long had finally happened. 'Now he's a dead bastard,' your mother said. She delighted in saying it and the same look came back on her face. I didn't know what to say. What can you . . . All of a sudden she wants to talk to me. Wants to sit down. None of that I-can-only-stay-a-minute stuff.

Says yes to a cup of tea. I asked her about you and your sister. I was worried. She said you were all right, asleep, she'd hear you cry if you woke up because she'd left the door open. I was vexed with her. Coming over like that. Wanting to talk after saying nothing to me for so long, expecting me to be there ready to mop up. I didn't let on I was mad. I nearly did. I was going to but when I poured the tea I thought about her letting me have you and I let go of it. Oh, I know I was helping her out, taking you; she was doing me no favors in one way. But soon as I saw you playing on the rug I couldn't be mad with her anymore. My, that wind's getting up."

She turned towards the door.

"Is the sausage pushed against it?" she said. "Can't see it from here."

"Yes," I said. "I put it there when I locked the door."

"Was a funny business was all that. . . . A lot dies with you. . . . You sure? There's a bugger of a draft."

"It's right against it," I said.

"Where's it coming from then?"

"Maybe it's the window."

"Fooh. Goes right through you."

She grabbed at her cardigan, squeezed it round her neck and held it there.

"She had a chance to stay on at school, you know," she said. "Her form teacher wanted her to but her father had plenty to say soon as the time came when she could leave. Told her she had go clean like her mother, what good were bloody books for the likes of them. Truth was he didn't want either of 'em to go to work. Wanted 'em stay home and keep house for him. But the money he got wouldn't run to that as well as keep him in beer. Nowhere near. He'd never have given the beer up. Was the one thing his pride came second to. She didn't go cleaning, but for a time, they made out to him she was. Her mother helped her, through a friend who worked there, to get her a job in the pottery. Secret didn't last long. Some geezer on his shift, coming up in the cage, said he'd seen his daughter at a bus stop in Barlaston the other afternoon but she hadn't recognized him when he waved. That did it. He put two and two together and got it out of them. He hit them both, her first, then her mother, made her mother's mouth bleed. Same night he went to bed early because losing his rag like he did brought his cough on bad. They even looked forward to his cough coming on, except for the noise, because it made him lie down. She waited in the front room behind the sofa, said she could still smell urine from when her grandma lived in there, waited until he'd been upstairs awhile, till the coughing stopped, when she knew he'd be quite weak, before she went into the kitchen. Her mother was sitting there facing the door, watching it. Her lip was swollen right up. She sat by her. Took hold of her hand, then whispered it all, tried to get her mother to help her kill him, told her they'd put up with this too long, she (her mother) knew; he'd never stop doing it while he had an ounce of strength still in him, she knew that too, always had, that she'd read in the paper of a mother and daughter who did it in self-defense, it'd be all right, that's what it was they'd be doing, defending themselves, they'd be believed, everyone knew what a swine he was, they'd get away with it. But her mother said no. She'd thought of it a million times, made it seem right, but now she said no. She wouldn't do that to him because she knew what he didn't know, or wouldn't accept, that he was already dying. The doctor told her, after the one time he was forced to go when he couldn't breathe, there was no cure for his lungs. He refused any proper treatment. Said he'd only gone in the first place to show her what a lot of charlatans doctors were. It was only a matter of time but the doctor wasn't sure how long. Said he could do something for his tuberculosis but not much for the black lung. She asked how the end would come. He told her the lungs would get so they couldn't pull air in, or rupture before they got like that, then he'd drown in his own blood. . . . Said the only way she knew to get even was let his own body turn on him; was the best revenge she could think of. She'd gone on helping him for years, doing for him, against his hitting. She was stuck with him, felt dependent somehow. But now when he was bent double gasping for air she didn't go help. She could just let him be or not be, she didn't care, because it was all the same in the end. And she knew the end weren't far off. I don't know if she'd have done it if her mother'd said yes. There was fear in her. You could see it the way she acted when she came over to tell me her father was dead. She couldn't believe it had happened after wanting to be rid of him for so long. . . . Sort of fear hate grows off. Same as what I had with wanting the baby so bad. You can't do anything. It takes over. It's both sides of the door. . . . If her mother had said yes she might have been different, got over the fear, who knows. . . . Like I said, what made it worse in the beginning was me seeing her pregnant. It fetched it all back when she came over about her father. She talked up a storm that night. Just that once, mind. Never opened up like it again. But even then there were little things. . . . Like how she talked, stopping in the middle of something then starting on about something else. Got me thinking she was still keeping things back. . . . Per'aps it was me. Could've been. I mean making her feel uneasy or something. I wanted that baby, her baby inside me so bad. I wanted it to grow in me, get big with it so they could all see it was mine, touch my tight belly, feel for themselves how drum-hard it was, that it was real in there, mine. Wanted it to kick inside me, remind me all the time it was alive and I wanted to see it come out with my blood on its head, girl or boy, not hers, mine. How good can you cover up something like that. She was too young, I told Harold, still a schoolgirl, what did she know about having a baby. He said she didn't have to know anything to have one, it was nature's way. I told him shut his face, what did he know about it, if it weren't for him I would . . . I walked out the house shouting 'Why should that bitch of a kid . . .' I'm sorry. Was wicked to think that, I know, but at the time I didn't give a shit for no one, I suppose, not even Harold and he'd never done me no harm. You know even now if I'm not careful it all starts up again, driving me, and I know there's no chance now on God's earth of me having one. Over six years since I had a period. . . . You asked me. . . . What d'you want me to . . . What you wanted to hear, isn't it. Pass me the soddin' bottle.

"She was a pretty woman. . . . Errch, what does that

matter once you're dead. . . . What did it matter then, tell me that. . . . Face you remember was older, but you could still see. It hadn't all worn away. . . . When she let me take care of you again I tried to forget all the bad feelings, and the bitchy things I'd said to other women about her. But it still came between us a bit. The baby, I mean. Had to, I know. Didn't say a word to her about the way I felt. I couldn't somehow. But she must have known something wasn't quite right. . . . And I liked to think it was her fault, not mine, that we didn't get on. You know with all of that I reckon it worked out all right in the end. Could have spoilt everything the way we were with each other, but it didn't. . . . Strange how we managed to find a bit of trust. Think that's what it come down to, a bit of trust. With Harold it was different. It's different with a man, in't it. . . . Blimey yes, that must have been it, a scraping of trust. . . . She wanted to stay on at school, told her mother that's what she wanted to do, but she knew she could do nothing about it, nor could her teacher, once her father said he'd kick her out the house sooner than have her stay on with that bloody book learning, earning nothing. Her friend Joan stayed on but her parents were different. They had more money, for a start. Her dad had a few taxis. Wanted his daughter to have the very best. All the things he said he never had as a kid. He was forever telling you how he'd built himself up from nothing repairing bikes in a shed. But I heard he had money left him. . . . So she went to work in the pottery. They started her off learning the painting. She got good at it fairly quick. Had a knack with it, they told her. She didn't see Joan after she started work. They soon drifted apart. Once her father saw she fetched more money home than cleaning would have paid he said no more about her working there. The more she could give her mother out of her wages the more he could take down the pub out of his was how he looked at it now. She went to work regular. She knew she had no choice but pay her own way. She did that all right but she soon became listless, began traipsing around when she wasn't at work, not seeming to care about anything. She was quiet, kept herself to herself more and more. Took no interest in things. When I asked her about school, was it having to leave what had made her like that, she just said she didn't want to talk about it. Her mother encouraged her to make friends, get a boyfriend even, not just wander off by herself all the time. . . . After a few months she was used to the work, but she still spent as much time as she could over the fields on her own, away from the house. What changed it was when the woman who sat opposite her at work left and another woman started. The new woman was open and warm with her, which the other woman never was. They got on. She lived in the village too. She was a few years older. I knew her by sight. Jenny Smitter. She don't live here no more. They got to talking in the first place on the bus one morning. Jenny persuaded her to go to a Saturday night dance at the church hall with her. Jenny was after finding a new fella. One she had before broke off their engagement and went with another woman. He'd been seeing her for over a year. He never told Jenny about it right up to the time he was supposed to go with her to see the vicar about getting married. She told Hazel there were plenty more fish to fry now she was over him, he could go fuck himself. She said they should both get themselves nice fellas to take them out then they could have some fun. Jenny got her in the way of dressing up, putting makeup on. She'd never bothered with any of that before. Her mother was happy for her, relieved, I bet, seeing her dress up, take an interest in herself. But him, the father, he went on about how it was sluts painted their faces like that and strutted around in them stiletto heels. So after he said that she always left the house with no makeup on and her high heels in a bag. Anything to keep him off her back, she said. She waited till she was out of sight down the lane before she changed her shoes and soon as she reached the lamp she pulled out her compact and did her face by it. Was at one of them dances she met Tom Thwaite, your father. He wasn't from Grebedown. He came from Riddon Moor to go to the dances. In them days there was a dance in Grebedown every other Saturday night. If he was there the first time she went she never saw him. But next time she'd not been standing on the side very long, waiting for someone to ask her to dance, when she knew someone was looking at her. She felt awkward but looked across without hardly lifting her head, saw the mop of curly black hair. She avoided his eyes but knew it was him looking and she turned away slowly. He came at her from the other side and asked her to dance. She told him no first. But Jenny prodded a yes out of her, so she was pulled off to rock and roll. Was all the rage then, rock and roll. Surprised me when she said she knew how to do that jiving. She'd learned it before she left school. Joan taught her in the playground. Her dad bought her all the latest singles. She

knew them by heart and sang them and showed Hazel
the moves. Joan could do the man's part as well. . . .
He danced with her a lot, kept coming back, asking her
for another one. After the dance was over first she said
no to him walking her home. But that Jenny, she could
do it when she wanted, put her up to it, said she'd have
to go with someone sooner or later so why make it difficult
on herself, besides he's not a bad-looking fella. Get some
practice, she told her. So she went with him. . . . That's
how it got started. . . . To think you only . . . He talked
her all the way home, to the bend in the lane, about
football, boxing, he was crazy about boxing, and cars.
You know what they go on about, men. Stuff she didn't
give a toss about. But she knew it meant he was interested
in her, least that's what she thought at the time, and with
Jenny encouraging her she soon got to thinking how
maybe it could be a way out. She didn't think about him
much though. Couldn't remember what he looked like
after he'd gone back down the lane, except he had black
hair. . . . He walked her home after the next dance, went
on about the same things. They'd gone to the pictures
the Saturday in between. She went stiff when he tried to
kiss her. Kept telling herself not to, she had to get some
practice like Jenny said. So she tried to go with it, grit
her teeth as he rubbed at her breasts, then she filled her
head up with running away across the fields to try to
forget what he was doing to her. It wasn't what she was
after was snogging but she was afraid to tell him stop.
She didn't know how many chances there'd be of getting
someone to take her away from home, didn't want to lose
the one she had, not now because she didn't know. But

when he squeezed her hard, hurt with his hands, she pulled away. He was annoyed. She smiled quick to put it right again and whispered to him touch gently, she was sore there. But he didn't know how. His hands were callous and heavy from the coal. . . . She had no strong feeling for him one way or another, would have liked it better if he hadn't tried to kiss her. . . . Whether she knew what Hazel was really thinking about him, Jenny egged her on every day, across the bench at work, saying he was a good-looking fella, he must like her to keep asking her out, there was far worse than going with a miner. . . . I'm right, I'm sure, Hazel saw him like she'd have seen anyone who'd come along. As a chance, half a chance even. She grabbed at it. . . . What did she have to feel in return. Nothing. She could have pretended, like a woman can, if she has to. Pretty easy is that, especially when it comes to letting them do it to you. . . . Christ knows I've clutched at straws enough bloody times to know that. Half the time you don't know why. . . . Wouldn't make much difference if you did. Not even a fool in a place like this would dream of her white stallion coming. . . . I'm telling you she knew what she was after. . . . You don't have to know about the consequences to be after something. Doubt we'd ever do much if we did. . . . It were never so bloody cut and dry as just running off, I knew that much. . . . Makes her no different from the rest of us though, does it."

She picked the bottle up from the floor, drank from it, then slopped some into her tumbler. She gave me the same distancing look as before and pushed the bottle at me. I took it from her. I held it for a minute as she stared angrily at me. I wanted to say something but there was no point. I stretched so I could put the bottle on the table without getting up again and I let it make a bang as I put it down. She looked back at the fire.

"If you think it's any easier for me you're bloody wrong," she said.

She took another mouthful, held it still over her tongue, then swallowed it with a glug. I didn't believe her. I realized now she wanted to tell me all this, probably had for a long time. She wasn't one for keeping things to herself. She hadn't needed prodding. She was devious. Far more than I thought. And I knew she could come the innocent when it suited her. For one thing telling me gave her an opportunity to feel sorry for herself. She reveled in that. Suppose it wasn't hard to understand.

"Your mother kept things from me all right," she said. "Don't mean just in hospital either. All along she was doing it. Buggered if I know why. . . . After all I done for her. I was the only friend she had at the time. . . . Beats me. . . . Took care of you for her, didn't I. . . . I don't bloody care. . . . Why the fuck should I, eh. . . . It grows . . ."

She shook her head, sighed, took a deep breath. She knew how to lay it on all right.

"After one of them dances it must have happened," she said after a while. "Back of some hedge. That's the usual place round here. . . . Doubt she said yes. He must have just took what he thought was his after waiting till then. By force, I bet. . . . Was no getting away from anything once she found herself pregnant. . . . The dreaming had to stop then, didn't it. There was no getting away now. . . . First off Tom Thwaite denied it was his, said he'd pulled his cock out in time, said she must have been two-timing him and went to hit her, but stopped when someone walked round the corner by the post office where they were standing in the dark in the rain, after she'd left a message at the pithead, saying she had to see him urgent. He said no more, just walked off. Kept out of her way after that, went to no more dances. She didn't know what she should do. She turned to Jenny. She said she'd help her get rid of it, told her come round her house on the weekend. . . . And there's me listening to all this wanting desperate again to have my own baby and not a soddin' thing I could do about it except have her tell me how she tried to throw hers on the heap. . . . Christ, I wanted to knock her over that minute. . . . Jenny gave her a bottle of gin, made her drink as much as she could get down till she was dizzy and sick with it before she undressed her and helped her into a hot bath, hot as she could stand it. Made her stay in the water while she boiled up kettles to get the water even hotter, then made her put her head under. But nothing came out. She waited a week, running and jumping and getting out of breath like Jenny told her. It'd worked for a friend of hers, she said. Still nothing happened. Then she tried on her own to do it. One night when her father was at pit and her mother was out she went up to her room and with her back to the door went after it with a knitting needle, poking in herself. Blood came but she didn't get the baby. She tried it again another night with a thicker needle but she couldn't get to it. . . . When her breasts had swollen and her belly was showing she had to tell her mother.

Together they went over Riddon Moor to see his mother (he had no father he ever knew). She said she'd talk to her Tom, that he'd listen to her and come to his senses. . . . So she had get married. . . . Even now seeing that needle makes me shudder. . . . Some things you never get used to. . . . They picked a time when they knew her father'd be home for Mrs. Thwaite to come round with Tom. It was Mrs. Thwaite told him there was to be a wedding. They thought it'd be better coming from her. Her mother tried to make the best of the announcement, got the best china out. When Hazel went into the front room to fetch a plate for the cakes her father followed her in there while the others were talking and slapped her across her face. Then he went back into the other room and said, 'Her's a good one, her is, son, c'mon, me and you's going fer a pint,' and they left the three women to the cakes. . . . Throw a lump of coal on, will you. . . . She told me they went to live at his mother's right after the wedding, and that first night when it was time for bed she put her nightie on over her underwear and held out like that often as she could until it was better than a beating not to . . . Makes me . . . Can't under-stand what it is with some people gets them like it. . . . I really can't. . . . Harold wasn't like that. . . . No. . . . Except he was no bloody good when it came to giving me a . . . What's the sodding point. . . . What . . . Tell me. . . . Don't know why I bother half the bloody time. . . . One fella doesn't change much on his own, you know. . . . Them slag heaps took years to get like that. . . . Generations of digging and dumping. . . . So don't let them give you any shit about that. . . . They go on piling

it up and up and up. . . . What for. . . . Why do they
go so high. . . . Baby'd get black as hell crawling in that
stuff. . . . Die. . . . It's no place even to shit in. . . . When
the baby comes on my life I'll never let her near there.
. . . He'll never get his hands on her, never. . . . It'd be
safe with me. . . . Safe from all that and anything he
was going to do to it when . . ."

She slobbered into sleep. I took the tumbler out of her
hand and left her there slumped in the chair, breathing
through her mouth. I went up to my room quietly but I
don't think I'd have woken her had I stamped on every
stair. The room was freezing. I got into bed with most
of my clothes on. I lay in the dark with my eyes open.
Nothing was changed. Her spewing it all out down there,
getting drunker and feeling more and more sorry for herself, changed nothing. I expected most of it. I just wanted
to hear it from the horse's mouth. What was I supposed
to do, start feeling sorry for my mother all of a sudden
for what she did. Just proved I was right, didn't it, soon
as she told me about the knitting needle. I don't feel for
her one bit. She had her chances like everybody else.
Why didn't she leave if it was so bad. She didn't have to
take it out on me and Susan. We never asked to be here.
It wasn't our fault. She never wanted us. Only interest
she ever took in us was pushing us to do well at school
and only that because it made it easier for her, saved her
from having to get close to us in any other way, and once
we'd left school and Susan had gone, there was still nothing between me and her but what was empty chatter. I
bet she named me Hazel, same as her, so that when she
had to call me she'd hear her own name, see herself first,

not me. The drunk downstairs was no better. She'd just used me. Steered the situation to her own piddling ends. I wanted to be sure I was right about that and I was.

I closed my eyes but then I got to thinking again there had to be some money. Just had to be. She'd probably hidden it. She didn't want me to have any. Whatever I found I decided to take and keep my mouth shut. It'd be small compensation but better than nothing at all. I don't know what time I eventually fell asleep but I was still thinking about getting her money when I did, and I remembered my dad's wages. Maybe I'd be able to claim them now.

The kitchen felt warm when I came down but all you could see in the grate was ash. She was asleep quietly. She hadn't moved from where I left her. I got the door unlocked and open without waking her. I tiptoed across the yard. I needed some time in there on my own if I was going to find anything and be able to keep it to myself.

Mother's door was on the latch. I tried not to make any noise closing it. The kitchen was tidy, the table cleared. I looked at the oilcloth again and wondered, had she lived, how much longer she could have made it last. I lifted it back so I could open the drawer. The cloth was brittle, cracked, about to crumble. I pulled open the drawers in the dresser too. I looked through the boxes and jars she kept in the cupboard; looked in the painted vase on the windowsill. No money. I stood still. Her clock was ticking its annoying tick. I moved round the room trying to think of other places. The nitid black edges on the range picking up light from outside caught my eye. I went over. I felt behind the flue for a sealed tin or box but there was nothing there but a layer of soot. I washed my hands. She used to black and buff that range once a week. I don't know why she bothered. It was an old-fashioned piece of junk.

In the front room I unlocked the cabinet that had come from her mother's, with her mother's china, when she died, and dipped in the cups and bowls and jugs. Nothing. The stairwell smelled musty. I hurried up the stairs. First I went into the room I used to share with Susan. It was empty except for two single beds, not made up, jammed against each other, and an old red rug on the floor. The man from the mission wasn't going to find much when he came to clear out the house, I thought. The cupboard had junk in it. I found the box with Susan's guide sash in and the school photos and my doll. The velvet dress had gone. If she'd thrown it away why didn't she throw the rest of the things with it. I couldn't understand why she hadn't. I didn't want any of it. Not now. Wondered why I ever did, what made me put them in a box in the first place. I didn't want to be reminded. I went into her room and searched but I couldn't find anything. I rocked back and forth on each floorboard to see if any were loose, looked under her mattress, poked behind the wardrobe. Nothing. In the small table by the bed, in the drawer with the broken handle, I found a plastic purse. All that was in it was a piece of paper torn from an exercise book. On it in her writing was written, "I know he'll come back, wont you Rosko you will wont you." It meant nothing to me. I knew no Roskos. She'd never said anything about a Rosko, but then she wouldn't have. I put it back in the

purse and closed the drawer. I went onto the landing.
Took the picture of the girl picking flowers by a stream
off the wall to see if there was anything hidden behind
it. There wasn't. I put it back. It never seemed to hang
straight.

I thought maybe Beth had been in here before me and
taken the money. She'd had plenty of chances before I
got there. I went as fast as I could through the smell on
the stairs and began over in the front room trying to think
of new places she could have hidden it. I was on my
knees feeling in the sofa when she made me jump:

"She didn't leave any."

"Any what?" I said. "Why'd you creep up on me like
that?"

"Money. That's what you're looking for, in't it."

"How do you know?"

"She told me."

"She told you?"

"Yes."

"What was it to do with you?"

"She told me she never saved anything."

"I don't believe you."

"Please yourself. But I don't see how anybody could
save on her wages with what she had to do with it."

"Nothing? The way she scrimped? Come off it. She
had more than enough."

"Maybe she put some in the post office. But it won't
add up to a hole in your pants, you can be sure of that."

"Where are the certificates? I didn't find any. I've looked
ev —"

"Could've been in her handbag. I took it to the hospital for her. Don't know who's got it now. You'll get 'em if they're coming to you."

"What do you mean?"

"Just what I said. . . . You going to take anything of hers?"

"What for, it's mostly junk."

"To you maybe."

"What would I want with any of this."

"I dunno but I'd have thought —"

"I buy new stuff. I don't want any of this."

"There's people who'd be glad of it."

"Man from the mission's taking it, you said. Did he offer you any money?"

"They pay next to nothing."

"What did I tell you."

"I left the kettle on. Are you coming? All you'll get in here's a bloody cold. It's freezing."

"In a minute."

"You're wasting your time, I'm telling you."

"Damned clock keeps going."

"They don't just stop when you die."

I waited for her to go then opened the back of the clock. Nothing in it. I stopped the pendulum. No more of that hollow ticking taking away the minutes. I looked in other places in the kitchen but it was no good. I couldn't find any money. It peeved me. I was sick of the place. Sick of ever having to be a lousy part of it. I grabbed the oilcloth off the table as I went out, scrunched it up, and threw it in the bin in the yard.

She was bending down in front of the range when I

opened the door. Between the tangles of her hair you could see the white of her scalp. She didn't get up or even turn round. I saw her push an empty Scotch bottle into the ash bucket until it disappeared. I was going to come right out with it, ask her if she took the money, but I knew then she'd say no, swear on Harold's grave she never touched a penny. I couldn't prove she had taken it so I kept my mouth shut. I sat down at the table. I wondered how much of what she said last night she could remember, wondered whether she'd say anything about it, or just let it pass as if it never happened. The kettle whistled for a good two minutes before she got up from her knees. I wanted to push her out of the way and take it off myself to stop the damned whistling. It was worse than the clock ticking. She made the tea but took her time about that too.

"I'm going to catch the twelve-forty train," I said.

"All right by me," she said. "Nothing to keep you here."

"You'll give the key to the landlord after they've done clearing out the house?"

"Said I would, didn't I. Here. Put your own milk in." She thrust the bottle at me.

"It'll have to go to probate."

"What?"

"Because she left no will it has to go to probate. Same as with Harold. They have to sort it all out. Before anyone gets a penny."

"Oh, that."

"I couldn't get my own money out the post office when Harold died. They tied everything up. Even though my name was on the book. Those buggers tell you what's what."

"They'll know if there's money then?"

"Suppose so. . . . If there is any."

"There is, I'm sure. Somewhere."

"Wouldn't count on it if I was you."

"Why shouldn't I? It'll come to me. There's no one else. Do you know anyone called Rosko?"

"Can't say as I do. Rosko. No. Why?"

"It's nothing."

"You wouldn't be asking me over nothing."

"It's just that I found a bit of paper with the name Rosko written. In her bedside table."

"You've got me."

"She never mentioned a Rosko?"

"No."

"It was her writing. Done a long time ago by the looks of it."

"Don't know what that's all about."

"Anybody ever come here? Another man, I mean?"

"Not as I ever saw."

She said she had to pop out, she wouldn't be long. I went upstairs to put my things in the bag. That didn't take long. I thought she was showing me the real side of her now. No more calling me chick, or asking me to do things with her. I went into her room and started to look for the money. I looked in as many places as I could think of. She had some pound notes and a couple of fivers in her dressing table drawer but not enough to make me think they were Mother's. She'd have hidden them better if they were, I suppose. I took a few of the pound notes just in case I was wrong and I was just about to search more when I heard her come in. I went back into my room as quietly as I could and picked up my bag.

"Hazel?"

"Just getting my bag," I shouted back.

I went down quickly to give the impression I'd only been up there a minute. I put my bag on the floor near the back door. She was undoing the head scarf she had tied under her chin.

"Still pretty nippy out there," she said.

She stuffed the scarf into her coat pocket, then tugged the coat at the back of the door to one side and pulled a bottle of Scotch out of the shopping bag hanging behind it. When I saw that bottle I was glad I was ready to get out of there.

"Just fetched it from the off-license," she said. "Have to have something drink in the house. Mrs. Rock usually comes over Christmas Eve before she goes to church and she likes a nip with her mince pie. You'll have one before you go, won't you."

"No thanks."

"Go on, it'll warm you up before you face the cold."

She went to get three glasses from the front room, and poured Scotch in two of them. She pushed one at me and sat down with hers in the same chair she slept in. I stayed by the table, sitting on the edge of a kitchen chair.

"She didn't want to get married in the first place," she said. "That's what I think was wrong with her. She never got over having to. She stayed angry. Never tried to get used to it. That's how it was with her, why she treated you the way she did, I think. You reminded her all the time of what she hadn't wanted. But she tried her best. She never wanted to be stuck with it. From the way she talked she was after something different. Christ knows what. Doubt she knew herself. Being stuck like that wasn't for her; then on her own with two kids to rear. That much were obvious when you look back at it."

"Why'd she put up with it then? Why didn't she leave?"

"What bloody choice did she have. Where was she supposed to go. You reckon she should have dumped two little kids and buggered off. Whatever else you blame her for she never did that."

"She might as well have."

"You don't mean it."

"Don't I."

"You don't know how it was for her then. Times is different now. She was young, I know, but —"

"Don't give me that. You took advantage of her situation, didn't you."

"Maybe I did but I was only trying to help."

"You don't really believe that. You should listen to yourself. Help who?"

"I do. I did you no harm. . . . This fighting won't get us nowhere."

"Maybe not. But it's true you were just out for yourself."

"When I saw she was having trouble coping on her own I tried to help is all I'm trying to say."

"She didn't want to cope."

"You can't say that, you bitch."

"I can and I am. She didn't care about me and Susan and you know it. Trying to make us do well in school isn't everything, but it was for her. Only thing she ever cared about when it came to us was school, school, more bloody school. You said the very same thing yourself last night if you remember. Do you remember?"

"I can't answer for her."

"I'm not asking you to."

She was finished her first drink, first I'd seen her have anyway, and was up after another one. These glasses didn't hold as much as her tumblers did, not even half as much.

"Why do you think she sent us up Holdworth's?" she said.

"Sent you up, you mean. I haven't a clue."

"Like to know what she was after, sending us up there."

"Don't think you would."

"What d'you mean?"

"Nothing."

"That's what you always say."

"I'd better be going. Don't want to miss my train. With these buses you can't be sure. Especially holiday time. We've nothing more to say anyway."

"Funny making us go up there like that."

I kept quiet knowing she wanted to carry on with it. She couldn't let go. I put my coat on. I'd more than had my fill of her now. Don't know how I'd managed to be so nice in the first place.

"Suppose I won't see you again," she said.

"If I need a lawyer to handle this I can get one in London so I've nothing to come back for."

"This isn't how I expected it to turn out."

She wanted to have us make up, but she had no intention of offering herself. I ignored her and picked up my bag. I saw no point in trying to sort it out and if she hadn't been feeling sorry for herself again perhaps she wouldn't have either. I opened the door to go.

"I've got your number if I need to get in touch," she said.

She followed me down the entry and watched me down the road. I didn't turn round, walked as fast as I could carrying a bag. I expected her to shout something after me but thankfully she didn't.

As I walked by the chip shop I hoped to God I wouldn't bump into Mrs. Blatt. She could turn up anywhere, anytime. The last thing I wanted was to have to face up to her. Thinking that made me hurry on again. I got to the bus terminus without seeing anyone I knew. I half expected Beth to come panting round the corner with something I'd left behind just so she could start it all over again, about going up the hill, or the money, or how she never understood why Mother did one thing when if she'd listened to her, had done what Beth told her, things would have been better for her. There always had to be something with Beth. Just had to be. She never let dead dogs lie.

It was the same conductor on the bus. He was quiet. He didn't dance. The bus stopped and started smoothly every time so there was no need. I think his regular driver must have been back. I hoped he would dance because I liked watching him. He was good at it. We got to the station in plenty of time. Most of the passengers got off before the station. Meant I'd have a better chance of getting a seat on the train.

I went into the canteen to get a warm drink and a sandwich. I moved a paper off a seat near the window, pushed some empty cups and plates to one side, and sat down. I looked out across the platform. Bits of paper were being blown around in circles. Two sparrows hopped between them, one looking more keenly than the other to see if anything to eat was moving by. A piece of red and green wrapping from someone's present, still shiny, was held flat against a side of the newsstand by the wind coming down the tracks. I thought, By now she'll be plastered again, that she'd probably made that up about Mrs. Rock going over. As far as I knew Mrs. Rock didn't like her and I couldn't remember ever seeing her at Beth's on Christmas Eve. If she wasn't asleep she'd probably be cursing me, or my dead mother, or Harold for leaving her childless, for making her appear the barren woman when it was him the barren man they should have been looking at. How I'd changed towards her. But then perhaps I hadn't. Just been keeping my real feelings about her, about them both, pent up till now, hidden away from myself too, most of the time. Why did I do that so much.

An old man in a tatty overcoat and shoes that were too big for him and coming apart at the sole came in and stumbled over to me and asked if I had the price of a cup of tea. I gave it to him. After all it was supposed to be

Christmas. Then I wished I hadn't. Don't believe in scroungers. He bowed, managed to click his heels without falling, and saluted. He was halfway across the canteen when he turned round and shouted, "God bless you, young lady, and compliments of the season to you from General Quicksalts." He edged along in front of the counter looking in the glass cases at the sandwiches and cakes, then as soon as he reached the cashier, he put his empty tray back on the pile while looking the other way. He walked furtively down the far side of the canteen and out onto the platform, the tea money still in his pocket. I finished my sandwich and watched him get the price of another cup of tea from a man with a trilby who he'd tapped on the shoulder and smiled at. He squeezed the money in both hands close to his chest, jumped off the ground an inch or so, then turned a full circle and saluted. The man with the trilby looked hard at his newspaper and pretended not to notice what the old man was doing. He'd paid to get rid of him, not for the show, and he probably didn't want the passersby to think he'd done either. When he'd bowed and saluted him again, and smiled with his head to one side, the old man turned on his heels, and shuffled off stiffly past the ticket office. I didn't see him accost anyone else. The likes of him ought to be made to get a proper job, I thought.

I took my ticket out, picked up my bag and made my way to the barrier so as to be in plenty of time. The man who checks the tickets was in his box picking his nose and humming. He didn't see me standing there at first. I could see the front of the engine and the cleaning crew coming along the platform with their brushes and rags and things, and black plastic bags full of rubbish. He dropped his hand quickly, fumbled for his punch, and said yes, it was the London train. He punched a hole in my ticket and said it'd be all right to go through, they'd done cleaning it. I grabbed a window seat and put my bag up on the rack. There were people standing when we pulled out of the station. Some of them started to move through into first class.

And I'd thought there'd be plenty of seats judging by the bus.

The train got up speed quickly. I had the feeling the woman sitting opposite wanted to talk. I'd had more than enough of that the last two days. She kept fidgeting and looking at me with a dozy smile on her face and then opening and closing her handbag. I turned well away and looked out of the window. Soon nearby fields and hedges were whizzing by so that cows and sheep seemed to be moving when they were standing still. You had to look in the distance to see how it really was.

I hadn't wanted to, but I was soon thinking about it all again. . . . When I stopped the clock I hoped that would be the end of her. But it wasn't yet. I could still hear the ticking and I was never able to separate her from it. Nor now. Time to do this, time to do that, was how it was with her. You could hear it from the top of the stairs, tick. She made us do homework by it. Made us go to bed by it, go to school and come home by it. Never let us get away from it. . . . I should have gone when Susan did. . . . If it was only the money to remind me of her I could put up with that till I'd spent it all. But the clock. She was always winding it up, making the time go, as if she was waiting for something special to happen that time would bring sooner. The train rattled through the afternoon as I tried to get it out of my mind. Beth says a lot dies with you. Not enough if you ask me. No.

Rosko

I hear the next ambulance siren. I look down the ward at the double doors again, just outside the Sister's office where they keep the controlled substances locked up. I keep looking. When the din stops I close my eyes. Tight.

Coming down . . . It's happening all over. . . . I'm coming down Parson's Road. Fourth gear. Bull and Starling on the right. Car park's empty. Well after kicking-out time. Clear night. Some moon. Stars. The cold whistles under my helmet. A cat scuttles back from the gutter into a garden. Carrying something. Looked like a bit of oily rag. Limp. A mouse it had teased the life from. Row of poplars on the left behind the council houses very still. Doing about forty miles an hour. Nothing coming towards me. Look in the mirror. Nothing. Signal anyway. Habit. Change for the turn. Reflex. Pass red pillar box. Then start left into Murphy's Lane. Blank. Always goes blank here. Right before I get hit. Blacks out. Blank. Then SMASH. Lasts a long time, getting hit does, before it fades, as if a picture of getting hit is held there. But there's no pain when the smash comes. Spill, slide. Feel nothing.

The nurse brings something to help me sleep. I get my

injection at the same time. She's very attentive. She only has one more person to see to after me. The man in the next bed. We're the only ones on the wall at this end. Paint down here's going to peel soon. There's cracking. Up the wall. Across the ceiling. . . . Three empty beds. Makes it a bit easier for the nurse having less of us in here. She says good night to everyone in a loud voice and dims the lights. I see her sit down in the Sister's office and start writing on the record sheets what she's just done to everybody; who's had what up 'em or down 'em. But she won't let you see what's written about you. Every now and then she looks through the glass at us dutifully. She knows she's good at her job. She doesn't make a big thing of it.

Getting drowsy. Starting again . . . Coming down . . . Try to think of something else to get my mind off it. It won't budge. . . . Coming down Parson's Road. Bull and Starling on the right. No cars outside. It's past midnight. Still. Some moon showing. Cold nips my face. Poplar trees behind the council houses on the left don't move. They can't. Doing about forty miles an hour. No faster. Nothing coming towards me. Nothing in my mirror. Signal. Habit. Change down. Go by the pillar box and turn into Murphy's Lane. But no blackout this time. Nothing smashes into me. *Hazel, one foot in the road, waving both arms. Hear her shout "Rosko" after me . . .*

There's a thermometer in my mouth and I'm being rolled over for another injection. The muscle in my bum tightens hard on the needle and aches. When the nurse is done shaking the mercury down, flapping both arms at once, I ask her how long they keeping me in. Not up to her, she says. Tells me to ask the doctor when she makes her ten o'clock rounds. It's only a few minutes after five by the clock over the door. Five more hours to get through, watching sickness. Doesn't go away if you take your eyes off it. The moans. You hear the moans. Some of them moan a lot. Wish I had a net here to mend. That landing net's got to be fixed before I go fishing again. Light outside. No cloud. Still feel a bit woolly-headed but I don't think it's anything to worry over. Want to get out of here. The smell gets to you before very long. Nurse says I'm to stay in bed. You can't argue with her. Not to get up till the doctor's seen you, understand. But I can have breakfast if I like.

Ten past seven. Must have nodded off. I can smell the tinned tomatoes on the food trolley down the other end. Never noticed before how they smell like piss. I lift the sheet. Look under at the leg. Nurse says it's quite a deep cut. There's blood soaked through the bandage. She tucks the blanket back and tells me the antibiotics I'm getting can make some people feel morbid. She checks my blood pressure. It's okay, she says. She's telling me things all of a sudden. She writes the numbers on the chart and hooks it back over the rail at the end of the bed. She walks off towards the Sister's room. The phone in there is ringing. Before she's halfway there she turns and says to me in her loud voice, same one she always uses, "You'll make it." Must think I'm worrying too much. The other nurse is dishing out the breakfasts. Piss-slopped tomatoes.

I can't tell if there's something wrong with me apart from the leg, whether I've damaged my head. No pain really. . . . I'm not hungry, I know that much. And I know I don't want to be in here. If I can just think about one thing. . . . But it's different with your head. You can't test it like you can your leg. How can your own head tell you if you're a little queer. It's not like a pain you can locate; if you've gone a little scatty there's nothing to feel. There's no way of you telling. Someone else has to tell you you're off your rocker. By then, though, it's probably too late. She did say the drugs can do it to you. Make you feel a bit strange. . . . But she could have said that to stop me worrying. I try to remember what happened, piece it together. But when I get to the minute, the second, before it hits me, it's blank again. . . . These painkillers make you feel good. . . . Maybe that's . . . If you tell yourself you're fine there's no way of knowing you are if your head's not right in the first place. You're snookered. SMASH. You all right? Don't try to move, they've phoned for an ambulance. What happened? Don't talk. Lie still. It'll be here in a minute. You'll be all right. . . . *Who wouldn't change it if they could? Have it how they liked it once? You sneered when I said that, asked me if I'd gone soft. Thought I must have changed a lot. What did you expect, Hazel. What . . .*

The same nurse wakes me up to tell me the doctor is making her rounds, that I must sit up, be ready. She says she is going off duty, thank God, soon as the doctor's been and gone. She folds back the sheet, pulls it tight across the bed, smooths the wrinkles out. I look down at the leg again. Is it festering? No more blood's come through. I've been sweating. The smock thing they've given me to wear is damp. I tell myself I remembered it was the same nurse. Head can't be too bad if I can remember . . . Just need to fill in the blank. See myself getting hit. She pulls the curtain round the man in the next bed. He looks very sick. No color in him. Like a powdered wig.

There are too many learner-doctors making the rounds for them all to fit behind the curtain, so after a bit of scuffling behind the consultant's back, five or six are left on the outside. They look knackered. One of them just stares across at the blood on my bandage and picks the tubing of her stethoscope. She's miles away. Some of the others put a routine ear to the curtain. . . . They're coming round anticlockwise. Will she pull the curtain round me, stick me in the Punch and Judy show? They don't always. The thin bloke down the other end with the big lump on his neck didn't have it pulled round him. Depends how much private poking they want to do, I suppose.

It's gone quiet. What are they doing in there? The nurse pushes her way under the curtain, flicks it over her head. She smiles as she comes over to me, then bangs my pillows into shape and tries to get the sheet even tighter across the bed. She lowers my leg. Moves it left. Then back again. Lets go of it. It's ready for them now. Curtain opens. They spill out, all in white, most of them with their heads down. Important buggers.

"Good morning. I'm Nora Wilson. They tell me you were knocked off your motorcycle. How are you feeling now?"

"I . . . Yes. I'm feeling okay now."

"Good. We'll just take a look at you to make sure everything's all right. First I'm going to give you three words I want you to remember. All right?"

"Is . . . Yes."

"Clock, butterfly, nurse."

She seems friendly but like I feared she suspects my head's messed up. Fella at work had it done to him. He couldn't remember the words and they kept him in. Clock clock, butterfly butterfly, nurse nurse. I can remember them. So far she's said nothing about motorbikes being suicide machines like I expected. If she did I was going to tell her I've been riding bikes on and off since I was fourteen so how come I've made it to thirty-nine if they're so bloody dangerous. It's not the bike. It's the . . . I don't think I'd have said "bloody" to her. The Sister's unwrapping the bandage. Her cold hands feel good on the hot skin. She's holding my leg just below the gash.

"I'd like you to bend your knee as far as you can," Nora Wilson says. "Good. Notice that he has full range of motion indicating all the tendons are intact. Do you see any signs of erythema, edema, or feel any warmth, Dr. Aruna?"

Dr. Aruna examines my knee. So do I. It's worse than I thought. Much deeper. I get a nasty tingling in my balls when I look at it. She feels all round the cut.

"No, I don't," Dr. Aruna says. "There's a little purulence, though."

"Any crepitance?" another doctor asks.

"Feel for yourself," Nora Wilson tells him.

He pokes about on my leg above and below the wound, round the back as well. When he's finished he tells Nora

Wilson he's found no sign of crepitance, so they move to my head. That's what she's after, I know she is. Nora Wilson tilts it back. Feels all right to me.

"Notice he has no periorbital ecchymosis," she says. "Remember, ecchymoses differ from petechiae only in size. They have different causes, of course. In American journals periorbital ecchymosis is often referred to as raccoon sign."

"Raccoon sign?" one of them says.

"Right," she says. "It's an important indicator. Do you see any evidence of a battle sign, Dr. Mostel?"

Dr. Mostel pushes to the front and looks behind my ears at my neck. She pushes me forward as she does it, almost leaning on me. The silvery buttons on her coat are colder than the Sister's hands. . . . *What did you put in your pocket, Rosko?*

"No, I don't," Dr. Mostel says. "Does this mean we can rule out a basilar skull fracture?"

"It's not absolutely foolproof," Nora Wilson says. "But in the absence of a battle sign we don't look for fractures unless something else strongly indicates it. So far there's nothing here which does."

I'm thinking about battling raccoons when Nora Wilson says:

"I'd like you to move your eyes from side to side and up and down."

I snap to and move them like she says. Makes me lightheaded but I don't tell her.

"Do you see anything double?" Nora Wilson says.

"No."

"Where are you?"

"Where am I?"

Dr. Aruna smiles.

"Yes, where are you?" Nora Wilson says.

"In hospital."

"What's your first name?" Nora Wilson says.

"Rosko."

"What year is it?" Nora Wilson says.

"Nineteen seventy-eight. Why?"

"Just a test we use to see if someone is oriented, to determine whether there's been any concussion, damage to the brain."

Another test. That fella said the more tests they give you the worse it is.

"What are the three things I asked you to remember?" Nora Wilson says.

"Clock butterfly nurse. Is that right?"

"Yes, fine," Nora Wilson says. "I think we can let him go home this afternoon. The nurse'll show you what to do with your dressing. She'll give you something to clear up that infection. We'll see you in outpatients' in a week."

They break away from my bed like part of an iceberg and float in one jagged piece down the ward.

I tell the nurse I don't want any lunch. When the others have had theirs and all the plates and things have been wheeled away on the trolley she brings me my clothes and says I can get dressed. My trousers have a big rip in the left knee. I have to make it even bigger so it'll fit over the bandage. Leather jacket's gashed too. The nurse tells me how to take care of the leg and gives me antibiotics and painkillers and a sick note for work. . . . *Why did you run away, Rosko?* I thank her for looking after me and push the door open to go. She says not to put too much weight on the leg, keep it up when I can. She gets me a stick from behind the door in the Sister's office. I smile at her. This time she smiles back. She tells me not to forget to bring the stick back when I come to outpatients'. Government property, you know. She smiles again. I smile back.

Once I'm through the door I practice with the stick, walking up and down, a few steps at a time, to get the knack of it. Doesn't take me too long. Just have to distribute my weight differently, not spend long on the bad leg. By the time I get into the lift I feel I don't need the stick, think about not taking it.

The only other person going down is a hospital porter holding on to an empty wheelchair. He's about fifty with a pencil mustache and plastered-down jet-black hair, and a beer belly stretching his shirt. He stares at my bad knee. I'm thinking he must dye his hair to get it that black. Tea leaves or something.

"What you been doing to yourself then?" he says.

"Got knocked off my bike."

"Motorbike?"

"Yeah."

"They're bloody death traps them things are. Oughta be banned. Bloody death traps. Just goes to bloody show, don't it. Used to do the ambulances, didn't I. Scraped enough of you young buggers off the tarmac. I oughta know. Took the pieces back in a plastic bag. Smell got to me in the end. Death traps, I'm telling yer."

He looks away mumbling, nodding in agreement with himself as he maneuvers the wheelchair so it's tight against the doors. He's going to be first out no matter what. The lift stops with a jolt. The doors don't open straightaway so he swears and rams the chair at them. When they open he darts out to the left, the wheelchair careening. He just misses this man coming the other way, who shouts after him, "What's the bloody hurry, we'll die soon enough without your soddin' help," and the man behind him says, "Nice one, son," and joins in and shouts, "Daft idiot," but the porter's gone, is out of sight. I follow the exit signs to the right and take it steady because the corridor is crowded. My head begins to feel clearer. There's a smell of ether. Amputations. Pieces of flesh in a plastic bag.

The hospital grounds are well looked after, especially the box hedges, which look as if someone used a plumb line on them to get them so sharp and upright. I find a bench by a flower bed and sit down. Feels good to be outside again. The clock in the gatehouse strikes the half hour. Plenty of time before the big race. I move the shadow of my stick along the ground fast and slow, and fast again, then off the ground I get it to touch the top and sides of the sundial, making a circle with it before I stop fooling.

The lupins stand almost still in the warmth, lots of different colors mixed in clumps spaced only inches apart. . . . *She was always after flowers: finding them; smelling them; touching them. She said you could hear them if you were quiet enough. The double daisy chain she made for me that afternoon after school while we sat in the field by the stream near the old bridge, I kept for years, long after it dried out, and when it eventually* turned to dust I put it all in a matchbox and sealed it. Her friend Joan wanted to come with us that day (she kept asking if she could when Hazel told her where we were going) but she wouldn't let her; she said two's company, and Joan mad as hell with her and red-faced walked off blaming me for Hazel being like that, calling me a shitty ratbag. Hazel never wanted her to come when it was just going to be the two of us together. She was hard on Joan sometimes but Joan always came back to her, back for more. Joan looked up to Hazel because Hazel would do things Joan was afraid to. While Hazel delicately threaded each daisy in turn through the stem of another I had to keep the horseflies from biting her, keep on swishing at them with a branch of alder I'd snapped from the tree on the bank just below. She said if her dad saw bites on her he'd know she'd been in the fields and beat her for it, for not going straight home. There were daisies growing all round us, more than enough, so we didn't have to move from the place she liked so much to look for any. This was where she wanted to be if she could, she said, where she wasn't afraid or ashamed, in the fields. It was a funny thing to say but I never asked her. What did I care then. I was watching her, her feet stroke the grass, her fingers nimble the stem, all of her smelling alive, as I waved the branch from side to side wanting only to be one of the flowers she was touching.

"You supposed to be sitting out here?"

I turn round. There's a nurse standing there waiting for an answer. She wasn't on my ward.

"They've discharged me. I was just enjoying the garden before I go. I'm in no hurry."

"Sun's a bit strong for you to be sitting in with no protection over your head. You've only just got out the hospital. What you do to your leg?"

"Cut it. Got knocked off my bike. Don't say anything. It's doing fine. It wasn't the bike's fault."

"All right, calm down. Just the same you shouldn't be sitting in the sun like this."

"Wasn't going to stay much longer. I'll be all right. Spent a lot of time in the sun when I was in the —"

"Don't blame me if your head hurts tonight. I warned you. Sun can be very nasty."

"Like I said, I wasn't going to —"

"Please yourself."

She marches off. There's always somebody to tell you what to bloody do. After a bit I decide to get going. I pull up on my stick, get to my feet. The bandage is on fairly tight so I can't bend the leg very far. No throbbing yet. Nurse said it could start anytime. There's an incline up to the main gate and I'm glad I didn't leave the stick behind when I start up it. I'm no match for a slope without the stick. The gateman tells me mind how I go and without thinking I lift the stick and wave to him with it. Bet he's saying to himself, Who's he fancy he is then, a bloody squire or something, cocking his stick to his beaters. I need to get a paper. I smell something as I go through the gate. It's not honeysuckle. I'd know that smell anywhere but it's a bit like it, sweet-smelling. *You made me close my eyes to see if I could smell the flowers you picked, one from another, and you sometimes gave me the same one twice and I'd tell you it was a different one. I* look round but I can't see what the smell's coming from. *You liked to catch me out.*

Two weeks off from work they've given me. Time on my hands. Get some fishing in. Leg should be up to that. See how the weather is. Maybe take a trip to the coast one day. There's a telephone box outside the gate. Phone's working. Bloody miracle to find one that does. I ring my boss to tell him I'm out the hospital and still kicking. He asks when I'm coming back and I say in two weeks and he says, trying to be funny, he thinks he's funny, how can they manage that long without me, and I tell him come off it, carpenters are ten a penny, he'll manage, and he says bring him ten then and he'll be glad to part with the penny and laughs down the phone at his own joke. He pisses me off. You never know where you stand with him; he wants to be one of the lads and the boss at the same time, and he's got to have the last word. Always. Never lets up. I should find another job when I get this leg sorted out. It's time I did. You get too set in your ways. Don't have to put up with his crap. I call the cop shop to find out where they took my bike and they say they want me to go down there to sort things out. Cops are all the same underneath.

I walk about twenty yards to the bus stop and lean on my stick, waiting for the bus. Two starlings hop along the side of the shelter, peck in a weed growing there. They run a few steps as the bus pulls up, then fly off. There are a few empty seats downstairs. The platform is higher off the road than I thought. It's tricky getting on. I get the good leg up first, hold on to the pole, then swing the duff leg round from the hip. The conductor sees the performance as he comes down the stairs, sees me drop the stick, and says he'll have it if I'm chucking it away, and picks it up. I make the step up onto the bottom deck all right with the gentle shove he gives me. I have to sit with my leg sticking out in the gangway. People are usually more understanding about bandages but I still feel daft having to sit with the leg out for everyone to see. I lean forward to try to see the racing page the woman in front of me is reading. I can't make out the names of the runners. She's got the paper folded. All I can read is part of a headline, "THE 199TH DERBY"; and further down part of another, which has "PIGGOTT" in it. I'm leaning as far forward as I can. I sit back and wait for the square where I can buy my own paper. I was going to anyway. *The look on her face when she opened her back door; as if disbelief itself proved I was there in front of her, after all those years gone home.*

"Where to, young man?"

"Square, please."

I give him the right money. He gives me a ticket and says with a smile:

"Don't drop that now, there's an inspector on my route today."

Out of the window: a large brown dog sniffing all round and up the arse of a small squat one with a brindle coat, hackles up on the brindle; a young woman pushing a baby along feeling for something in her shopping bag as she goes; a postman down on one knee emptying a pillar box; a young kid trying to light a fag cupping his tattooed hands; two old geezers, dressed up, fob chains and all, sitting on a low wall looking straight ahead talking, and my guess is they're talking about someone they know who's just died, and counting those they know from the old days who are still alive, wondering whose turn next without putting each other's name forward, not today anyway, when they've already got a funeral to go to.

It's my stop. The conductor helps ease me down off the platform. Not half as bad as getting on. Wish he were still alive so I could kick his bastard head in. Linden Bastard Sapper.

"Mind how you go, young man," he says. "And if you change your mind about that stick you can leave it for Brian at the depot. With this job I'll be needing a good strong stick before long."

He laughs.

"Thanks," I say. "Be glad to get rid of it."

He rings the bell and the bus pulls away.

I walk across the square towards the newsagent's next to the New Inn. An old woman, bent double, is feeding the pigeons in the middle by the fountain that never has water spurting out of it. Whenever she shuffles or throws down more grain the birds, there has to be a hundred of them, all at once flap into the air, and make a semicircle with a swoop, never bumping into each other. Looks as if they've been practicing. What with the way they land together, neatly, and make their way, dipping, to the food. Here they come again. They're landed. A cockbird gets halfway to the corn, forgets himself, and starts to display to the hen bird in front. He puffs up his chest, and as he goes round and round like that, throwing his head up and down as well, gobbles and coos expand his neck. When he takes a break he sees the hen is pecking corn, ignoring the show. He doesn't try her again. As I hobble by, three or four birds, away from the main group, leave the ground, then drop as suddenly on the same spot without seeming aware they ever took off. Smart birds, pigeons.

Ossie shuffles along behind the counter to get me some rolling tobacco and fag papers. *It made her cough when I got her to try it in the hut. I had a packet of Park Drive with five in. Never again, she said. She went white with spluttering. I said "It's good when you get used to it," but I couldn't make her change her mind.* He keeps the tobacco in large glass jars with screw tops. I don't call him Ossie but I know it's his name. Everyone knows it's his name but only old people call it to his face. He was awarded a medal in the First World War. Everyone knows that too. He likes to talk about it. Remembers it as if it was yesterday, he says. He's got his own little war now. It's become a scandal with some that he hasn't changed his shop inside or out since the day he started in it God knows how far back. Before the other businessmen in the square began harassing him to modernize to fit in with them he'd get it painted once in a while, but not now, he says. They are trying to get some legal action taken against him. He laughs at them and says his newspapers are as up-to-date as anyone else's and his tobacco fresher because he's the only one round here who keeps it in jars.

I pick up a *Daily Mirror* from the pile on the counter and give him the money for everything. He wants to know what happened to the leg and when I tell him he says he was a dispatch rider for a while in the army and came off more than once and got cut. I'm opening the door trying not to make the bell clang too loud when he says:

"What do you fancy in the Derby?"

"Shirley Heights," I say.

I back into the shop a couple of steps, stuffing the tobacco and papers in my jacket pocket. Ossie leans over the counter and looks up at me. His bushy eyebrows form a canopy above his horn-rimmed glasses.

"He's too lazy," he says.

"But he never knows when he's beaten," I say.

"He will this time. Admirals Launch is the horse."

"Admirals Launch. True, he can come on at the end but he'll never get the trip at Epsom."

"Get on with yer. He's by Brigadier Gerard."

"Yeah but he's not got the —"

"Going's firm, you know."

"Won't stay the distance all the same. Shirley Heights won the Dante."

"That's nothing to go by."

"C'mon, right after the Dante Starkey said 'I'll win the Derby on him.' He ought to know."

"Means nothing. Piggott says he'll win. Means nothing. You need the right horse. Admirals Launch, I'm telling you. Got to have the right horse."

"I've got it. By Mill Reef out of Hardiemma. What more d'you want."

"You trying to tell me he's as good as Mill Reef. Get outta here."

"All I'm saying is he's got the edge in this field."

"You young'uns never listen. I was studying the horses

before you was ever a twinkle in yer mother's eye. Horse, Admirals Launch. Jockey, Willie Carson."

"I'll give you odds."

"Couldn't take your money. Be like robbing a baby."

I get halfway to where the old woman is shaking the last of her corn from a brown paper bag when I remember I've no matches left. I go back and Ossie gives me a box of Swan. "Fresh out of England's Glory," he tells me. I dig in my pocket for the difference. "Be some in tomorrow," he says, and against the clang of his bell shouts, "Admirals Launch, I'm telling you." He's always out of England's Glory. Like the rest of the country these days.

I walk to the far side of the square where it's shaded and sit on a concrete bench. From the exposed ends of the metal ties streaks of rust run down over the gray. Some of it comes off onto my bandage. It doesn't look like blood from close up. I'm dying for a smoke so I roll one up and take a few drags before I check the runners in the paper. A cloud covers the sun. For a minute. Then all the shadows come back one at a time, quickly, and it's warm again. *I just stood there looking at her in the doorway seeing the years past on her face. Gone over it a hundred times what I was going to say but the words deserted me. Stood there like an idiot. After all that time, like a bloody idiot. Should never have gone back. But then . . .* I feel the vial of tablets in my pocket as I put the tobacco away. I pull it out and push the cap off, look at the tablets, shake them. It's not hurting now but I wonder should I take one in case. Not sure I'll be able to swallow it without a drink, they're pretty big, so I put them away and roll another cigarette instead and light it and hold it in my mouth while I turn to the racing page.

I look through the Epsom card and read what the tipsters have to say. Nothing to make me change my mind for the Derby. Shirley Heights has his supporters but all of them agree it's a wide-open race. I need two more horses for a treble and I go for Bell-Tent in the Daily Mirror Handicap for one. Nothing else I fancy running at Epsom so I look at the Ripon card. Blimey. Sapper Stakes. That were her name before she married, Hazel Sapper. Married. I pick the six-to-four-on favorite, Irish Display. Sapper Stakes. Bugger me. The old woman isn't there when I put the paper down. Most of the pigeons have gone too. I finish my cigarette, stub it out on the concrete end, and manage to flick it first go in the litter bin. I roll up the newspaper. Sapper Stakes. A regular punter like me should've come across that before. Think I'd have remembered if I had. But you never know.

No clouds in sight. The going'll stay firm. I look to see how much money I've got on me. More than I thought. Five pounds is what I had in mind to put on a treble. Seems a lot now it's come down to it. I count the money again. Adds the same. If I lose it'll just leave me enough to get by on. I've had longer odds. Like they say, if you don't put any money on you can't win and somebody has to. That bit of it isn't true unless you count the bookies. They're the real winners. Odds in their favor every time. Cold, calculated odds.

A stir of the wind pushes against leaves on the plane trees making the ground underneath mottle, and the mottle move. I stand up, still using my stick, and think about what I stand to win on a five-pound treble. It's a tidy sum. As I pass under the trees the light mottles over me too, but faster than on the ground. *What did you run away for, Rosko?*

The betting shop is full. Three men, in white overalls and Wellingtons, from the dairy round the corner, are leaning on the narrow shelf, which runs down one side of the room, writing their bets. One can't get his biro to work. He blows on the end and tries again, pressing hard. He shakes it. It doesn't work. He scratches at the paper until it tears but nothing writes. The biro is attached to the back of the shelf by a piece of string. He grabs at it, pulls hard, but it doesn't break. He throws the pen at the wall and says "Fuck it," and waits for one of his mates to finish writing his bet. The place is full. Mostly men, standing and smoking, listening for the uninterested voice to come back on the air with the start of the next race, the off, waiting for the charge they've paid for. A few, just big-race followers, you can tell, scan the pages from the racing papers pinned round the room, skip from one to another, looking for a clue to a winner, then mill about hoping to get a tip, hear someone say he knows a stable boy's brother, or his dad, anyone as long as he's an inside story to tell. The old hands don't read them like that, regular punters don't twitch, they blend into the place like woodcocks. The boy who writes the odds on the board climbs up his ladder, rubs out the last-race runners, then stretches over to the Derby list and chalks in the latest odds. Julio Mariner is current favorite, six to one. Above the cashier's counter something, no one can make out what, comes over the air, and the thick crescent of smoke that was hovering in front of the Tannoy swirls up to the ceiling, as if it was the grunting voice blew it there. I find a biro that works and write out my bet then nudge my way to the counter trying to keep the leg out of trouble. The woman punches in my bet and gives me a slip. I've seen her before somewhere. Think she used to work in the off-license on Lear Road. The man next to me is holding a tenner in his tarred hand. He looks down and tells me I ought to be off that leg and I say "How long you been a doctor, what business is it of yours," and I make my way back to the door after I've put the slip in my matchbox. Nosy bugger.

It's not far from here, the garage where they took my bike. I know a bloke who works there. He drinks in the pub over the road from where I live. He's a biker and an ace mechanic. He'll do a better job fixing it than anyone. I can make it there and get back to the Dog in time to see the big race. I roll another fag and before I light it I look at the betting slip. Sapper Stakes. *She used to be so lively, full of everything, giving.* The man in the office says my victim's round the back, don't get any hopes up. So he calls them victims. Touch of a poet he fancies himself. He says Fred, the bloke I know, has gone to lunch. I walk along down the side of the workshop to take a look. Wrecks fill the yard. New arrivals squat in the middle, walled in by rusted shells and frames piled ten or more high. There's hardly any room to get fresh ones in here. Two cars, beyond one of the piles, way back of the yard, their windows and lights bashed out, are pushed halfway through the hedge, and have weeds and bushes growing in them. The rubber tip at the end of my stick won't purchase on the oil. I walk even slower. *Jumping the teacher. Putting fireworks through old man Sproat's door. Fixing the herring under Mr. Blessed's chair in the classroom to drive him mad with the smell he couldn't find where it was coming from. . . . Then. Why wouldn't I want then back. But it's gone. I know. It's now you want her.* My bike's tucked round the back of a Cortina with a caved-in side. Wonder if that's what hit me. The bike's a sorry wreck. Don't get my hopes up is right. Nothing Fred'll be able to do with that. They'll be lucky to get any parts out of it. I see I've got some grease on my bandage. Makes me think of Nora Wilson's raccoons.

A blackbird lands on the boot of an old Humber Super Snipe sticking out of a pile about five cars up, pictures me out of one eye, turns its head the other way, then to me again, and with a backward flick of its body shits, white, splat on the bumper, and is gone. I look back at the bike and wonder how come I'm not a goner. I touch the twisted handlebars, run my fingers over the chipped tank. There's red paint mixed with the green. Could've been that Cortina over there hit me. I remember I need to get a claims form. Those insurance buggers take forever to pay up when they owe. On the way out I ask the man in the office to tell Fred I dropped in. He says for sure they'll condemn my victim. Then he tells me he thinks I was lucky I wasn't hurt worse. People are always telling me things I know.

The wind is getting up stronger. Could mean a slow time in the Derby. Wind never changes the outcome like the going can, is what the old boys try to tell you. But if this keeps up it'll slow 'em down all right. . . . *Blew warm, strong over the island. Blue-green billows. Coconut palms twisting from the ground. We'd docked on Nossi-Bé for a cargo of bitter oranges and oils for perfume. Tied up a day ahead of time. Went ashore. Billy Filmer and me were together most of that voyage. We drank the dark rum they made on the island and that night, pretty pissed, rolled out of Hell-Ville and along the shore. Billy Filmer sang. He had a good voice, sang in a male voice choir when he was home from sea. It wasn't so good when he'd had a skinful, sounded harsh even to my drunk ears. Partway through a Welsh song, at the top of his tenor he stopped sudden, looked over his shoulder, and off balance said, "What in the hell's that?" "It must have been a bat," I told him, "or a nighthawk." "Big fucker, I'm telling you," he said. With all the booze he was still scared by it. "Things that fly in the dark," he said. "Always have been. Stupid, I know." He stayed quiet. He put his arm round me and we walked on aimlessly until his fear wore off and he said "I'm going in." He stripped off and ran and danced in the surf where the moon dangled and lit it up, and he sang, again in Welsh. Round and round he swirled in the churning foam until he tired dancing and dropped his arms to his side, and stood, the breakers dragging him in and out, before he forced away from them and walked up the beach and lay next to me on his back and said catching his breath, "You can never tell it how it really is, can you, just how things are." Then he said he wanted to do it and asked would I do it to him so we arsed each other and still salty from the sea he kissed me when we'd done, and fell asleep. I left him there and*

*walked down by the breakers, further from Hell-Ville. It
was always easier when we were locked at sea. It was
easiest of all with Billy Filmer; we were good mates. But
it never mattered if I was doing it to him or him to me,
I thought of her. Not with her clothes off or anything.
That's not what it was. After when it was just her to think
about on my own . . . always after when you wish you
hadn't, when you need the lies. I sat near the hissing froth.
The sand shone silver. I picked it up in handfuls and
watched the grains roll over each other and fall through
my fingers back to the beach. I remembered what Billy
said about telling it how it is, and thought, Lies work.
Most of the time they do. I stared out beyond where the
waves started to form and saw the slag heaps, and the big
wheels turning, pulling up the cages. I watched into the
night. They went up and down, lifting men, lowering
men, until I couldn't distinguish anything from the faceless water because the swell and shaft had merged. I got
up, looked away, and tried to will her out from the forest
behind the palms as I walked back to where Billy Filmer
was. By the time I reached him I'd begun to dread the sea
too.*

As I come round the corner to the Dog I hear this
woman tell someone "Fuck off." Then I see the man,
with his shirt hanging out and his donkey jacket torn
across the yoke, propped up against the pub wall. He tells
her "Fuck you," but doesn't look at her, stands there with
his head between his outstretched arms swaying, and
breathing so you can hear. She lunges at him, pulls him
away from the wall and bashes his head and face with

her fist and handbag, calling him a fucking prick, and he just struggles to stay on his feet, staggering. He's too drunk to get his arms up to fend off any blows. He falls and she kicks him on his way. He tries to get up. She takes off a shoe and starts to hit him with the stiletto heel. "You lousy fucking rat," she shouts, "you gave her my money, spend your own fucking money on the whore, cunt." She kicks him and walks off, putting her shoe back on as she hops and scrapes along the pavement, swearing, her handbag swinging wild from her elbow, hitting her. He groans, gets to his knees, waits on them trying to balance himself. It takes him a couple of goes before he gets to his feet. He fumbles with his fly as he sways. Too late. He's already pissing himself. Undeterred, he totters toward the bar door then lurches left, the same direction the woman went in. He tries to keep himself going straight and upright, but he can't, while shouting abuse after her, put one foot steadily enough in front of the other. He stumbles to the ground. From his damp heap, between grunts, he curses. I go over to help him up but he tells me, "Go fuck yourself up a piss-pole," so I leave him to it, miserable sod. I go in the pub.

"Still out there, are they?" Les the landlord says.

"She's gone," I say. "But he's going nowhere yet awhile."

"Not bloody surprising with what he got down him. Started their nonsense in here, slagging each other off. She wasn't far behind him. No bloody amateur was her when it came to putting it away. Pint?"

"Thanks."

"Heard about your accident. How's the leg now?"

"All right. Should get the stitches out next week."

"Thought I'd have more in being market day. Never bloody know in this game."

"Yeah. Quiet, that's for sure."

Les's Great Dane trundles in behind the bar and barks so deep I feel it vibrate my ribs. He tells the dog to piss off. The dog cocks its ears halfway up and barks again louder. Les shakes his fist and shouts "Piss off." This time it lollops away. Leaves a reasty smell behind.

"Cops are going to do that fella who hit you. He was well over the limit when they breathalyzed him."

"First I've heard of it. Not been home yet. Only let me out the hospital dinnertime."

"One of the sergeants from the station comes in here. Not a bad fella. He was telling me about it. You'll have to make a statement."

"I know, I just called them. All they said was to go down there. Shouldn't lose my no-claims bonus if they do him. D'you know what won last race at Epsom?"

"Bell-Tent won. What's the hurry?"

"I'll have another pint. Have one yourself. That's one of 'em in. Had a treble."

"Bit early for celebrating, ain't it."

"Could soon be too late. Have one."

"Why not. Thanks. What you done in the Derby?"

"Shirley Heights."

"Done Shoemaker's mount meself, Hawaiian Sound."

"Mmm."

"Liked the name. Cheers. It's got as much chance as any other bugger."

"Cheers. You're probably right. Got to sit down. Give the leg a rest."

"Watch your horse get beat in comfort, eh."

"Come off it. First Ossie gives me a hard time, now you."

"What d'yer mean?"

"Shirley Heights. Don't say I never told you."

"Ah. We'll see. Didn't know you was such an expert."

Three men I haven't seen before walk into the bar. I sit down. Push my stick under the seat. Corner to myself. I slide along to get a good view of the TV. Les seems like he knows them. But then he can make it seem like he knows anyone if he wants to.

"What'll it be, lads," he says.

"Four pints of bitter," the one with the cap says.

"Be on in a few minutes," Les says.

"We'll have mild then. Don't matter."

"Derby, I mean," Les says.

"Oh."

Les starts pulling the beer. The one in the cap leans on the bar, gulps at the first pint pulled, and watches the screen. The other two go to a table in the opposite corner from me. I roll another cigarette. *Who wouldn't change it? Remember waves pound innocently instead. Plow up the sand. Scatter the slag heaps. Take it all back.*

"Did you have bet?" Les says to the fella in the cap.

"Not me, mate," he says. "Know bugger all about horses. Arthur has. Fancies himself a bit of a punter. Hey, Arthur, what you done in the Derby?"

"Inkerman," Arthur says. "Piggott, who else."

The cap puts his empty glass down, pays, then carries the three full ones over to the table, where he sits down facing the others, his back to the TV. Les turns up the volume on the TV and goes through to serve someone in the lounge. As the expert on the box is telling us what they've done in their three years, what they could do, should do, and probably will or won't do today, the thoroughbreds are paraded round the paddock in full view, forehead to fetlocks. I finish my pint and walk over without the stick to the bar to get another one. By the time I get there Les is back and he fills my glass.

"Going down well today, is it?" he says.

"Telling me. Nothing like a couple of days on the wagon to get your thirst up."

"How bad's the bike?"

"It's a write-off. Don't tell me, I know I was lucky."

"Going to get another?"

"Yeah. No reason not to if the money comes through."

The horses begin to leave the paddock.

"Nearly time for the reckoning, eh, young man," Les says to me.

"You'll need time for that," I tell him.

I try to get back to my seat without spilling any. One shaky patch where some slopped over the side. *Dirty bastard did that to her.* Not much wasted. The cap takes their empty glasses up to the bar. Orders three pints this time. Wonder why he does all the carrying. Maybe he's not paying. Les looks at the screen between pulls. You can hear the sound of hooves beat the ground as they canter towards the starting gate. Willie Shoemaker on Hawaiian Sound fills the screen.

"Fine-looking stallion, that," Les says.

"Watch Piggott," Arthur shouts across. "You wait."

More thunder of hooves. The latest odds flash up.

More thunder of more hooves. Inkerman canters; in close-up, Piggott looking stern, intent. Formidable middle right, cantering, ears pricked, ready to bolt, held on the bit, lips splayed, saliva. Another odds update, superimposed on a ticktack man. Goblin shares the screen with another outsider, Orange Marmalade. Cut again. Someone from the crowd is asked why he's here. Christ, they ask some dumb questions. Then he's asked what he's put money on. He says English Harbour and sniggers and waves at the camera with a "Hello Mum" sign. Cut. All twenty-five runners milling around the starting gate. Some, twitchy, tails swishing, jerking their heads back, flouncing sideways, lash hind legs at the air. Horses sweat up. Grass lush green. Going officially firm. Loose rein for the moment. Ex Directory walks behind Obrazovy neighing. Roland Gardens walks in front of Obrazovy, shows his teeth and rears up. Obrazovy backs off fast giving his jockey a start. Roland Gardens is brought under control. Settles down. A look at the crowd (thousands of little heads in the distance), the home straight, the finishing post, the odds again, back to the start. A new voice starts as the camera moves about. "Epsom Downs looks a pic ture. Epsom Downs home to this great contest since 1780, in which year Edward Stanley, twelfth earl of Derby, putting his money where his interest presumably was, founded the Stakes. For three-year-olds. It was over this the most famous strip of racing turf in the world that Mahmoud carried Charlie Smirke to the post in 1936 in 2 minutes 33.8 seconds, a record that stands unbroken to this very day, the fastest-ever Derby time. An amazing 2 minutes 33.8 seconds that those who look to time to determine quality will have their eyes on this afternoon. It was here sat kings and queens to watch such noble thoroughbreds as Never Say Die, St. Paddy, and Sir Ivor prove their class. It was here over this magic course that the great Nijinsky danced past the rest of the field to popular victory, and a year later in 1971 the majestic Mill Reef finished fast to put the issue beyond doubt, his pedigree and stamina triumphing to silence his critics. . . ." Voice is cut off. Good job. Blaa blaa blaa. Horses. Horses walking. Horses standing still. Horses behind horses. Tension. Being led into the stalls. Some refuse to go. Nostrils flare. Horses back off, rear up, quiver. Whip on the blindfold. Turn them in a circle. Another one. Blindfolded they go in. Most of the time. Heads whipping from side to side. Lather of sweat is focused. Zoom in to salty froth on chestnut neck. Flicked off by the rein. Shove the rest in, let's get going. Snap the gates shut. Pull the blindfolds off quick, you've fooled the horse. Pat him. Try to calm him down. They're all in. Kicking. Bucking. Say something to the jockey in the next stall to take some pressure off. Doesn't matter what, he won't hear you. All set for 199th Derby. Under starter's orders. Wrong. Hold it. One more to get in. Looking for him. Over on the far side. Camera's got him now. Focus. Follow him in. Blinds on. Push. He's in. That's your lot. Goggles down. Check your stirrups. Bend forward. Ready. Gates snap open. They're off. Bunching up straightaway. Mashing of hooves towards Tattenham Corner.

The leg starts to throb. I try to ignore it. Tip back the rest of the beer. *Like to throttle his poxy neck. Linden*

Bastard Sapper. Need another. I sidle to the bar. Les fills me up without taking his eyes off the screen, slops it over the side. They round the corner. Far from over. Anyone's race yet.

"C'mon, my son," Les says.

I'm trying to pick out my horse. There he is. Not a bad position. Into the straight. Hawaiian Sound is coming on.

"C'mon, my son," Les shouts. "Get in there. Hey, what'd I tell you. Hawaiian Sound or what."

Hawaiian Sound is in the lead. Arthur comes over to the TV to see where Piggott is. He's nowhere. Shirley Heights is still in there.

"What the fuck," Arthur says.

"Told you, didn't I," Les says. "C'mon, my beauty."

They're coming to the furlong marker. *Cut the fucker's prick off. Make him wear that on his lapel down the pub. That'd stop your dirty tricks, hey, Mr. Sapper.* They're past the furlong marker. It's Hawaiian Sound. It's Hawaiian Sound Shoemaker's not easing up any. Looks like he's got it in the bag. Hawaiian Sound is going to win it. But here comes Shirley Heights. Putting in a spurt. Starkey banging the whip. He's coming on strong. He's gaining ground. He's catching him. He's going to . . . but he's left it too late. No, he hasn't. He's still coming. He's not beat. He's coming again. He's something left. He's going to take him. They're neck and neck. Neck and neck. It's Shirley Heights. At the post Shirley Heights just got him. It's a photo finish.

"Holy Christ, that was close," I say.

"Bloody robbed," Les says.

"What a finish," I say. "You've got to admit he finished great."

"Shoemaker bloody had him," Les says.

"Horse was beat and you know it," I say. "Watch the replay."

Slow motion shows Shirley Heights just edge in front. We wait for the official result.

"Fuck this for a game of soldiers," Arthur says. "Some bastard fixed Piggott's mount. Oughta be a stewards' inquiry, I'm telling yer."

It's official. Shirley Heights by a head. Shirley Heights wins the 199th Derby. Arthur bangs his glass down on the bar. The other two get up from the table seemingly as uninterested in the race as when they sat down. They all walk out, Arthur last. He's trying to tell the other two it's a freak result. Piggott should have won easy if the horse hadn't been nobbled. The cap holds the door for Arthur.

"C'mon, you," he says. "That's last of my money you get to throw down the shitter. I must be going soft in the head. You don't know a horse from the hole in yer arse."

So the cap had the money. Why didn't he make the others fetch the beer? Les pulls me a pint. Tells me again he was robbed but says it's not so bad because he's got something to come off his each-way bet. Arthur comes back in. He's forgotten his paper.

"Got a dead cert in the next race, lads," he says on his way out.

Final odds come up on the screen.

Les smiles when he sees his horse came in at twenty-five to one.

"Bugger me," he says. "Look at that Remainder Man. Third at forty to one."

"Someone must have had it each way," I say.

"You're doing all right, mate," Les says. "Two winners at eight to one. What's your other horse?"

"Irish Display, Ripon."

"You'll be sitting pretty if that comes in," he says.

He goes through to the lounge bar. I roll another cigarette and take two tablets. Hazel Sapper Stakes, I say to myself when he's gone. I hear him lock the door in there. He comes back into the bar, pulls two pints and brings them over to where I'm sitting. He sits down next to me.

"Don't know if I can manage another," I say.

"Get it down you," Les says. "It's your last chance. I'm closing up a bit early. Got some business to sort out."

I'm struggling the beer down, he's telling me how time's never your own when you run a pub. He knocks his pint back fast. While I'm taking a piss he empties the ashtrays and puts the glasses on the bar. "Mind how you go," Les says as I go out the door. Outside I'm feeling a bit light-headed. It's warmer. The wind's died down. I make for the canal. Takes some concentrating. Why not lie in the sun. Sapper Stakes is a late race. It won't be on the box. I can get the result off the radio. Got to pick up that insurance form. It can wait till tomorrow. Everything can.

Next to a clump of dock leaves by the side of the towpath, below the steelworks, just above the goods yard, there's a patch of grass with no chip papers or broken glass on. I ease myself down with the stick. I take my jacket off. See another gash in it. Not worth repairing now. I watch a patch of oil float on the water, its boundary move and change making the colors over its surface overlap and shimmer new colors. I'm still watching it when these two boys ride by on bikes and one of them says, "What you been doing to your leg, mister," and his friend says, "Got it bit by a mad dog," and he sniggers at me. The wheels kick up dust from the path as they pedal towards the lock. Some settles on the oil and dulls the shine on it. *Why did you run away, Rosko? Why did you . . .* I turn round at the clanging. The ground starts to rumble. Tons of sparks shoot up. Below the light burns so fierce it looks like they've trapped part of a sun behind the corrugated sides of the smelting house. Spluttering clanging hissing all at once. The hissing, distinct, gets louder. Steam spurts through the metal sides. The light fades; long before the hissing stops and the steam's disappeared, it's eclipsed. Heat like that. Makes you think what you're made of. I fold my jacket, lie back and put it under my head and close my eyes.

They stop their bikes by dragging their feet hard on the ground. I keep still and squint at them. Same two. Before the dust settles one of them turns his bike round and moves off quickly sending up more. He's soon back again and stops next to his friend, who hasn't once taken his eyes off me. They're both looking at me now.

"Hey, mister, have you ever done it with a girl?" the one who's been staring says.

"Tried to do it with his leg, look," the other says and laughs.

"Shut up, idiot," the first one says. "Have you, mister?"

"Pretending he's asleep," the other says. "Look at him. He's never sleepin'."

"What's it like then, eh?" the first one says. "Tell us, mister."

He comes nearer with his wheel. Almost touches me with it. If he does I'll break his spokes for him. Ram my stick in there.

"Do your eyes stop seeing like they say soon as you get it in?" he says. "Do you shake like a jelly when you're doing it?"

The other one snaps off a stalk of hogweed.

"I think he's a loony," he says.

He throws the hogweed on me. I can't chase them so I leave it there.

"Told you, didn't I. He don't move. Loonies don't do it with nobody."

"Sometimes they do," the other says. "I've seen it in the paper about loonies. They lock 'em up for it."

He pedals off to catch his friend up.

I wait till they're out of sight before I sit up. I throw the hogweed off and roll a cigarette, light it, and toss the match into the canal. It's out before it hits the water. A freight train, with an engine back and front, grinds into the goods yard, pulling and pushing itself slowly across several sets of points as it twists its way. When I can't see it anymore I listen to it shudder on to its destination, until it pulls up with a long ascending screech, then a creaking, which reverberates between the sidings, making it appear it took much longer to stop than it did. I stub

the cigarette out, lie back and put my head on the jacket
again.

I'm not the best judge.
Someone had to know, one way or another. So I asked
around. It didn't take long to find out she still lived there,
that she'd been married but now lived on her own. I
knocked on the door. It was the wrong door. The woman
said I wanted number seven. "If she's not in," she said,
slurring, "she's just popped down the shop, she'll not be
long, she's never gone long." I knocked on the door. No
answer. There was lace across the window. I couldn't see
in. I went back down the steps to the road and dawdled
through the puddles towards the Cock and Turtle. But I
wasn't slow enough. I stood outside. By the church clock
there were a good fifteen minutes before opening time. I
crossed the road, unlatched the gate to the graveyard; it
closed behind me, barbarous on its spring. The rain was
warm against my face. It tasted fresh, made me feel clean.
Must have been the first time I'd been in there during the
day. I knew it only by night; the summer hours I'd spent
after dark looking for owls or waiting for the ghost that
was supposed to haunt, the ghost of a woman they said
had been buried upside down. I knew the shadows in there,
what to expect when there was a big moon, or wind, how
to go on black, cloud-covered nights. At dusk, as nightjars
churred and twisted above the graves, the smells always
changed; made me feel part of them, brought me in close.
Night always attracted me more. . . . Like they say it
does, everything looked smaller than I remembered, a lot
smaller. The stone church with its stone steeple, with its

graveyard, sloping fast away on all four sides, looked harmless now as I touched it, not gobbling up the sky anymore, not dwarfing me to an ant. I walked between the nearby tombs; the engraving on most said less about who lay there than the size of the headstone did, just where and how ornately it sat on the hill. I went with the slope, weaving between. The graves further down were much simpler, closer together. The names were gone from many of them, all that was left a stump of stone. I wondered who some of these people had been, dead so long, how they'd managed to make ends meet. Ours are ordinary lives, I thought, but we don't have them in our hands.

I came across Alice Sapper's grave in the longer grass by the wall with the yew tree growing over it. There were weeds on her grave. Didn't have to mean she was uncared for. There'd been a lot of rain.

ALICE SAPPER
b.1909   d.1974
Aged 65 Years
R.I.P.

was all that was written in the stone. He wasn't with her, Linden Sapper wasn't, nor in the next grave. He had to be getting on in years, I thought. He was quite a bit older than she was. Never knew why but both of 'em had something against me, tried to stop Hazel seeing me. But then the way your chin looks can get some people against you. . . . As I left more and more tracks in the wet grass between the graves, I looked for better words to say to her. The ones I'd brought with me had begun to sound stale, empty yet.

I didn't knock loud enough. Not sure if I made any noise at all. Second time she heard. She opened the door slowly, awkwardly with both hands, as if she wasn't used to doing it. Silly for me to say she'd changed, or she didn't look quite like I remembered or something. . . . From the first glimpse it was her all right. She asked me what I wanted, if I was hawking stuff she wasn't buying anything today. My guts tightened. She waited behind the door and was about to shut it when I stumbled something out like, "Remember me, Rosko." Having to recognize me, make me who I really was, aggravated her. I saw the anger cross her face and felt stupidity cover my own. Me being there was wrong somehow, and I knew the same minute I saw that, I should have left things as they were, kept to myself. That way she could be with me: she always had been till now. We stood there silent, looking at each other, shifting the confusion between us. In the end she said:

"You'd better come in."

She let me pass. The range shone, the kitchen was spotless and tidied away. She moved about so gently I imagined she was trying hard not to be a part of it. She put the kettle on. Time it took to boil wasn't enough for me to pull my words together. They'd gone. The lot. I darted all over: back to when we were kids; ahead of time, pretending; back to her kitchen watching the blue flame under the kettle; to her mother's grave denying somehow as I ran my hand over the wet stone that I'd end up like her, under the ground; to the bus coming, anticipating, hoping, all the way here. She put the teapot on the table and sat opposite me staring at it. She can't have known what to expect, and what I wanted to say, but couldn't without making a bigger fool of myself, was neither did I, I just realized. Has to be more than time's done this to us, I thought. You can't blame time. Truth was, as she waited for the tea to brew, she didn't want me there. I was making it worse for her. She looked up, across, hard at my eyes.

"Why did you come back, Rosko?" she said.

I went this way and that trying to tell her. Got nowhere. So I started to make things up to ease it on myself, but she wasn't listening. She did not want to know. For her just then there could be no good reasons for me going back, not one; was to have me struggle that she made me try to give some. And the minute I stopped she asked me again just as hard:

"Why did you come back, Rosko?"

I started to tell myself (what she already believed) there wasn't much sense in what I'd done, in what I knew one day I would do, ever since I ran from this place; but like a daft ape I came at it again from the corner she'd trapped me in, started making more excuses why I couldn't go back before. With her eyes on me that callous I soon dried up. She wouldn't let go.

"What did you put in your pocket, Rosko?" she said.

When I told her, when I found out what it was she meant, the miniature mouth organ (I'd lost it somewhere at sea), she seemed relieved. And disappointed. What had she thought it was? Hoped for? What did she imagine that she remembered so long? Such a tiny thing. I said I played it when I was on my own, that's all, most often, those days, when I sensed that fella my mother was having it off with was going to give me another hiding, because when I played it, somehow it made me less scared of him, and I knew it took some of his fun away when he saw that I was. Nothing strange about doing it, I told her. She said that all the time I was getting it from the tin I kept my back to her, trying to hide something from her. She saw it shine before I stuffed it in my pocket as some sunlight caught its metal sides. She couldn't understand why I hadn't shown it her, told her what I had. She said there were no secrets between us, were there. That surprised me more than her remembering the mouth organ had. I said there was no secret in it. It was never a secret. And the way the hut was I couldn't have done any different; with the shelf tucked in behind the door I had to stand the way I did. She didn't believe me.

Who measures silences . . . I was about to say I'd better be going, when her eyes softened. Nothing I said had changed her. I knew that. Perhaps she'd remembered another time and found something she could let go over, forgive me for. I felt it. The tightening in my stomach loosened then. I waited a bit. Then I put my hand across to touch hers, to try another way to let her know.

"Don't, Rosko," she said.

"Only wanted to touch your —"

"What for?" she said.

What for. What for. What . . . I stood up. I felt myself start sweating again. I grabbed the door latch.

"Rosko?"

"What?" I said without turning.

"Rosko."

"Was a fool thing to do, come back, I'm sorry," I said. "I'm off."

"Wait . . . I never told anyone about the hut," she
said.

I could see now how she thought I'd let her down by
putting the mouth organ in my pocket like I did, without
showing it to her.

My leg feels hot under the bandage, throbs. I move it.
Settle it down in a new place and roll a fag. I lie back
smoking while the lowering sunlight dances over the bud-
dleia a few feet along the path. I haven't heard the hooter
in the steelworks yet. Has to be near knocking-off time.
Martins are circling high above, fluttering their wings
then sailing awhile, then fluttering them again, and sailing and sailing.

I turned to face her. Loosing my rag wasn't going to
help anything. I'd learned that much. Told her I always
knew she would keep it a secret, and in the same breath
I asked her if she'd go for a walk with me. Had to settle
it one way or another, I thought. I'd come this far.

Without saying anything she got up from the table and
put her raincoat on. (I hadn't taken mine off.) I looked
at her for the first time without having her eyes on me.
As soon as she was aware of what I was doing she turned
away and moved by the range. She tied a scarf round her
head. Then she turned and prized a tile from the side of
the range. There was a hollow behind it. She put her hand
in, pulled out a tin, pushed the lid off and took a fiver
from a wad of notes in it.

"Don't like to leave the house with nothing on me," she
said. "You never know."

As we were passing the post office it started to rain
again, heavier than before. I thought she'd want to turn

back but she said, "Let's go to the water mill, there's never anyone there." She walked quickly. Pepper's field had no cows in it. I said, "Let's cut across that way." She said she had no special way of going. We climbed the wall.

"No cows," she said.

She landed first. After I jumped down I caught the end of her smile. She walked ahead making for the copse in the center. I didn't know what I wanted then so I tried not to steal anything from the smile.

The rain began to drive across the field in fierce columns. Forced our heads down. We made the copse, scrambled over the metal railings, and waited against the oaks for it to ease. Was no drier in there but the trunks took most of the sting off the wind. Buffeted, with water running through her sodden scarf and down her face, she seemed less troubled than she was in the house, yes, less afraid almost; but if she was afraid I didn't know what of.

First I hear sniggering. Then snot move in a nose. I know it's both of them back when one says:

"Mad bugger's talking to himself. Listen. Told yer, didn't I, he's a fuckin' weirdo. Talking to himself like loonies do."

Behind me. Never heard them creep up. I grip my stick, roll over, push up fast as I can on the good leg, lunge. The stick misses the nearer one. He gets away. But before the other can turn his bike round by the bush I ram the stick into the front wheel, thrash it about hard, holding it with both hands. I break some spokes. He struggles the wheel free of the stick and runs off carrying the bike shouting, "You'll have to pay for a new one, you crazy mad bastard, my dad'll get you."

Let him soddin' well try. He has to run through the dust his friend's bike kicked up. The hooter in the steelworks belts out. I lower the stick, slacken my grip, turn the other way.

Is it any better after a couple of beers, I ask myself. Just makes me look at things different. Doesn't stop me thinking about her. . . . I don't want to be here when the men come by from work. I break a tablet in two, swallow the pieces without water. Do the same with another one. Leaves a bitter taste. The lock gates are closed. Saves me having to walk further to the footbridge. I edge across the top of the gates. The wood is dry, makes it easier. At the other side of the canal I ease myself down the grass bank into the goods yard. I cross over tracks, pass rolling stock that's rusted up, abandoned; one metal container standing in a patch of dandelions now says UINNESS in faint letters along its side. I make for the wasteland beyond.

Across in Deepfields two bulldozers are crawling over the top of tons of garbage, squashing it, leveling it, pushing it further. When more rubbish is carted in and dumped the bulldozers growl louder under the rack of diesel fume, judder into line, and turn on the pile, ramming it, one seconds after the other, ramming it. Black-headed gulls circle and scold the relentless machines with their harsh kwarring. They follow the dross to the edge, mad after it, diving nearer and nearer the brutal blades, and as soon as cans, cartons, rotting vegetables, newspapers, and bones are pushed over they scavenge disagreeably below, until a fresh load comes in.

My leg stops throbbing. I take the path to the disused

quarry. When I get to the runnel there's a lot of water
in it. I forgot I'd have to cross it. No chance of jumping
with this bandage. . . . Not going back now. I pick the
shallowest-looking spot and stride through wide as I can.

I suppose one day they'll fill the old quarry in too. I
walk round to the right (only one way in) and sit on the
same ledge I always sit on, near the water. I look at the
water. It's not a blue, nor a straight green. Blue-green
doesn't fit it either but it's close enough. It's light, striking
almost compared with the rest of the drab round here,
very light considering how deep it is, and clear too. I take
my shoes and socks off. Give them a chance to dry out.
My feet feel warmer out of the shoes. There's none there
now but sometimes pochards rest on the water, and wi-
geon. Once in a long while you see someone fishing.
I've never fished here but I've heard they're there for the
taking. Too bleak here for most to fish, I suppose. But
there is something about the place. The desolation. I
keep coming back. I roll another fag. I'm smoking too
much but it's not so easy to give up when . . .

"Come back," I think she said, "come back."

*I put my hand out to do it again. Went to touch her
as she climbed the stone steps to the grain room above the
waterwheel with half its paddles rotted away. Moved to,
but couldn't, pulled back the hand before it could touch,
before she saw. It was not my place, I knew, but I wanted
it to be, to have her make me part of it, of her, longing
till it started to turn foul inside me. I stood harder on the
lichen, squeezed more water from it. When I could stop
wanting to harm her I followed her, up the mossy steps.*

The room was protected, still dry. It'd been patched up

and used for storage after the mill shut down, but was now abandoned. She sat on a pile of sacks in the middle. She'd taken her scarf and raincoat off by the time I walked in, and was warming herself, rubbing her arms up and down her sides. The blanket of dust covering the floor was ruckled in places with our footprints. Unwanted clues. She looked up at me. I felt more bedraggled than I was, when she asked what kept me. It made my body seem distorted, clumsy, without familiar limits. I knew she was aware she could do that to me, make me feel like this. I didn't answer, waited for her to ask again. But she didn't ask again, not this time. She said there was no shame in not wanting to go down the pit. She'd never thought there was any shame in it. She saw no special virtue being a miner, risking your life for a bucket of coal, for a lung of dust, going down because it was expected, taken for granted you would, like your father, when you were near enough a man, so as to make you one. It was a tough job, yes, very, had to be done, but where was the honor in that. . . . I'd got it wrong about her. Some of it anyway. I made a seat out of some sacks stuffed in a window ledge. Mouse droppings rolled off them. I could see no tracks so the droppings had to be old. Besides it was barn owl territory now.

Whether she made up her mind to as we were crossing the fields or whether it was being in that desolate mill made her tell, I don't know. I can't say for sure if I remember all she said. But I remember enough.

Could be the pethidine mixed with the booze's making me light-headed, worse than when I came out the pub, woozy. They said nothing, I don't think, about not having drink with the tablets. Some of them can do this if you mix them with . . . Water ripples from the breeze. It is moving. Makes the water look darker. Not me moving. Dizziness'll pass. Close my eyes for a bit. Moving me now. Toppling over the water. Open them. I'm sitting right where I was. Spinning. No fishing today. Dizziness'll pass. Her mouth soft as a feather. Spins slower. To kiss. Hear the water. Please say yes. Drop into the dark. Muzzy. Top of my head heavy. Pushing down. Stop, stop. Open them, it's better. Try to keep them open. It is. Keep them open. Watch the water move. Fix on one spot. Fix by the edge jutting out. The white edge where the water laps milky. Keep it there lapping. The sea. This water. No. Indian Ocean it was. Dropped anchor. Spices. After your money in the docks, after anything they could get their hands on. Got it without touching. You couldn't see them till it was too late. Their black lines slinking away, a shade-darker thief. Gone when you turned. . . . Hold still. Mutiny. Land now, you salt. . . . Shirley Heights by a head by a head by a head. No dead heat since 1884. Had a treble, didn't I. By a head. Hazel won't. Wait. Kiss. I came back for her but . . .

Him. *He was always* him *to her, her father was. Talking about when we were kids is how she got started on him. Him, Linden Sapper. Swarthy him from the grimy pit. When she said* him, *her eyes stiffened, stayed fixed like that till it was all out, or till she couldn't talk anymore, I wasn't sure which. I looked down at a patch of unbroken* dust, thought how many times she must have whispered this to an empty room, how many.

For years, she said, she went on trying to remember the first time Linden Sapper raped her. She believed that if she could, her imagination would have nothing left to feed off, so she'd be able to cope better, unblock herself some. But she stopped trying when she knew she wasn't going to remember, when she let it sink in she had to have been a baby when he started at her. It changed nothing. . . . He raped her mother too. It was rape with her because her mother never wanted him near her, hadn't since a few weeks after they were married, when she first saw the dark side of him reveal, first felt the strength of his fist in her kidneys and the back of it across her mouth. There was nothing in no marriage contract about none of that. But he took anyway; hers were not wishes to be respected. His wife belonged to him as far as he was concerned, and he owned her as debauched as he fancied. . . . Her mother found ways of suffering him, of explaining him away, but she never did.

He would come at her all sweet Hazel, then, the minute he saw she was refusing his lust, threaten her into the bathroom, where he'd force her to the floor while he wrenched at her skirt with his hard sooted hands. As he raped he'd tell her he thought her mother was a whore the way she put herself out for people; he'd mouth obscenities (even once he cursed his foreman into her ear) till the dust began to run like ink down his coal-shoveling frame, till the vengeful white had oozed out of him, when she'd crawl from under him, often blackened on her blouse, which she'd hurry to change and wash, him growling what would happen to her if she told what they'd done (THEY. Christ.), made her swear not to tell, then moaned he loved her, she was his own flesh and blood, his little sugarplum.

It was hard for her to say, when she must have known all along deep down what he was doing to her, why it hadn't hit her till her periods started, till she saw the blood the first time. Only then did she know, realize with her whole body, in a surge. Before that, before she had a word for it (rape was a flower), she somehow prevented it intruding on anything else she did. There was the hatred she could feel for him at the surface when she wanted to but the rest she made vague to herself, refused. The way she was so full of everything then, so lively, open . . . No one could have suspected a thing. And her mother did her best to cover up his regular violence. But that was something Hazel talked about, a lot of us kids did: My dad'll give me another bloody hiding if I . . . My dad's a nasty bugger when he's been down the pub.

Knowing changed nothing. She told herself it would get better now she'd faced in the open what he'd done to her, taken from her, denied her. But it didn't. Knowing wasn't easing. She became sluggish, lifeless. She couldn't understand why. Her old self never came back. She went to the doctor; she could find nothing wrong with her, a little underweight maybe but no anemia, everything tested normal, nothing physical to explain how she was. She didn't say anything about her father to the doctor when she'd done examining her and asked "Is everything all right at home?" Dangerous to, she knew, but she very nearly told her, only a nurse coming in with a syringe at that moment

*stopped her, prompted the "Yes, everything's all right. . . ."
The steam she'd had for Miss Carter, the bounce for each
and every day before, had suddenly gone. She stopped
deliberately hating him (that much changed) because the
need to incite revulsion with words was gone too; now
when she saw him or thought of him her throat gagged
and her stomach turned. And though the resolution was
there, to try to make the best of it now, it was limp, weak.
It didn't drive her, wouldn't. She wanted to do things no
more than she did not want to. And faced with choices,
however small, she had trouble making any. Circumstances
dragged her along. She couldn't care even when she
tried to.*

*She put an end to it herself. . . . Coming along the
lane from school one afternoon she met her mother carrying
food in a basket. She was taking it to the pithead to give
to them on the picket line. The dispute was beginning to
pinch the miners now strike funds were thinned out. There
was no extra money to give, she said, but she could always
stretch food further. She couldn't not support other families; with what her family had been through over the years
it was in her blood. Hazel was worried her mother would
get into trouble at the line because they all knew Linden
Sapper was a scab, that he crossed the line every day to
go to his cushy job as a surface worker (he couldn't go
down to the face anymore on account of his lungs). "They
don't see Linden Sapper when they see me," her mother
said. "Besides he's not from this village." Hazel asked her
what if he saw her taking the food. "I'll make sure he
don't," she said. "It'll be all right. He knows he's lucky
he's not got worked over for what he's doing. It's only on*

account of his being sick he hasn't met with some accident. Scabs usually get what's coming to them." Hazel wanted to go with her to the colliery gates but she sent her on home. "I hope they forget about his lungs and mash him up," she said to her mother as she walked away. She'd not been home long when he walked in, dirty off his shift.

"Did you see Mum?" Hazel asked.

"What do I want see her for," he said. "You's looking pretty today, young lady. How about making your old dad happy then. He's had a rough day with them commie bastards down there. There's only a handful of us men working, you know."

He'd called at the pub, she could smell. That's how they'd missed each other, him and her mother. He took his cap off and pushed his hand against her breasts. She moved back. He started to cough, coughed till he bent double. When she was certain he wasn't going to stop for a while she upended a chair and ran at him with it, legs first, knocked him to ground. He crumpled easily. Spluttered to the floor. She let the chair fall on top of him.

"No more," she said. "No more. No bloody more."

He lay there coughing and hawking, unable to raise himself. She ran from the house surprised at what she'd said and done. She knew, as she roamed the fields frightened, that by overpowering him and ending his rape, she had not washed herself clean of him. It was a small consolation to have him realize his strength was finally gone; but it would never be enough that he was no longer a threat.

I looked up at her. I was going to say something, prob-

ably curse him, not that it would have done her any good. But she didn't notice, didn't stop.

Alone, early one evening she remembers going up Marshes Hill to pick bilberries for her mother to make a pie. Not too long after I'd run away, she said. When she had enough bilberries in her bag she stood up, was ready to make for home but a skylark caught her attention. She put the fruit down. She slowly climbed over the stone wall and crouched at the top of Holdworth's field. It was a field she hardly ever went in. The bird was walking down the hill towards the farmhouse, aware she was there, apparently not afraid, not in any hurry, because it stopped, turned back towards her. She tried to keep very still, watching its thin pale legs. After a few more steps the skylark took off quivering its wings, and began to trill, and soared to a speck in the sky, where it hovered, then circled its continuous warbling, oblivious. She lost sight of it. She looked across the vale towards the colliery. She was aware the moment she saw the steam and the big wheels turning he was still on his shift at the face, and that's when she felt it for the first time, a release, as if from herself, away, a safety of flowers, to the fields themselves, their scent, and an excitement moved through her body, slow then fast, tingling fearlessly as she pushed her fingers through the swarth, part of it for now, almost whole, as the sun began to close and the lark fell, silently.

A week later she went back up Marshes Hill, climbed the wall into Holdworth's field at the same place, at a time she knew he was deep underground. When she looked over to the pithead the feelings returned, as powerful as they had been the week before. She only described them, made no attempt to explain. She found they would come back if she knew for sure he was down at the seam, and she could see the pithead. They did not always come back with the same intensity. It was better than nothing, she said very matter-of-fact, being able to do that, have those moments of herself, sometimes free of him, whenever he was at the mine and she went up to Holdworth's field.

She was twenty, with a daughter three and another only a few months old, when her mother went round, stood on the step and never went in, told her her father had died, only sixty-one, his lungs, like the doctor said they would, had finally done him in. Said they were burying him in Gorton where the rest of his family lay, Thursday two o'clock. Hazel said she didn't care what day nor what time, it was shit they were burying, she wasn't going to no funeral of his, her mother ought to know better than ask. Her mother told her hold her tongue, not to speak of the dead like that. Hazel said, "He was shit alive, and now he's dead shit, what's the difference." She didn't care if they took him to the knacker's yard. Her mother scolded her, got nowhere with that, then tried to persuade her to go to the funeral, asked if she didn't have an ounce of love in her for him somewhere. Hazel said she had to be kidding, there was more in stones. The morning of the funeral her mother went round, all in black, again to try to get her to go, if not for him this time, then at least to keep her mother company, give her side of the family some support. Tears dropped behind her veil as she pleaded. They didn't help persuade. Hazel was at home when they lowered her father's body into the ground for the last time. . . . "Linden Sapper, rot in hell," was the last thing she said before she went quiet.

Why did I think Linden Sapper was still alive when I was standing over her mother's grave in Grebedown. Odds were he'd go first. With working down the mine and all. Plus I knew he was quite a bit older than her. Dirty bugger had been dead fifteen years when his wife passed away. Funny, I . . . Must have wanted him alive so I could cave his fuckin' head . . .

Yes, she did go quiet, just that one time, after she said he could rot in hell. I remember she kept staring in the same direction, behind me. She became more intense and her eyes widened. It was as if she could see him there, all of him, come back alive, threatening. I turned round. It was a cobweb torn from the beam, hanging by one or two strands, she could see, tangled in a draft. Imagination had got the better of me. She was probably asking herself should she tell me any more.

She did. About her husband then. Part to rub it in, I bet. Tom Thwaite. Tom Thwaite . . . Fuck it. What was done weren't my fault. Half the time you get sucked in whether it is or not. That's other people all over. . . . Jealousy turned to anger at that. At having to be forced back; to press hard against the past. Nothing I can do about it. It's done, gone, all what made the difference is . . . It's now I want. Not then. But saying it, no matter how, won't change a soddin' thing.

I looked back at the unbroken dust, about to score lines across it, kick it, but her starting again made me grudgingly admit things had to be worse for her as she heaved the rest to words. So I sat still. For a time desperate to mash the dust with my boot, spoil it . . . Her lips had a tremble in them as she spoke. I love you but it's no help to you, is it, I didn't say out loud.

"I had to go to work with what Tom Thwaite put in me," she said. "Leave the house with it. Had to bring it home with me on the bus, then take it to work again and paint with it in me alive, growing bigger every day, because I couldn't get rid of it. I did everything Jenny Smitter told me to: gin then a hot tub (she took me to her house to do it); squirted salt solutions in me; tried to poke it loose; I ate weeds. Nothing worked. . . . This woman down the bench from me in the factory, Mabel, she was called. She'd been there longer than anyone. She had it in for me. I'm sure it was because I painted pottery faster than what she could. Well, she noticed first I was swelling. She got up from her work, came and leaned over me and said patting my back, "Cock'll have its way, won't it, luv, you can't be too careful, can yer, these days." After that, what she'd do whenever I stood up from the bench was stare at me down there, smile exaggerated at it, showing her teeth, then turn away saying nothing, smug on her face. She didn't have to say anything. She knew I wouldn't forget in a hurry what she'd said to me that one time. Bitch. She was always on the lookout to do someone down, pin some dirt. Gave me the creeps. I knew if she knew she'd tell others, and them she didn't tell would soon see for themselves. No one at our house had noticed yet. I knew I couldn't hide it from them much longer. I went straight home after work scared. I knew if I ran from the bus there'd be no one in. The house was quiet when I opened the door,

not even the tick of the clock reached me. Everything was in its usual place but nothing seemed familiar; it didn't smell the same was what it was. I didn't wait to account for it, just hurried, tried to go faster. I took two of my mother's knitting needles from her box under the stairs, wrapped them in some paper, then walked across the fields to Marlowe's Wood and hid in there. I waited huddled on the ground afraid someone would find me. I could hear my fears pounding. But when I was sure I was alone, after I'd calmed down a bit, I unwrapped the needles. They looked strange with dappled light on them against the leaf mold. I picked up the thin one. Rolled it over my clammy fingers from hand to hand, thinking I was always repelled by his touch, Linden Sapper's, I mean, because from the first I could remember, it was always rough, heavy, with his maggot smell following. I pushed the thin one in first, lifted my legs against a beech trunk and poked. I closed my eyes. The bark was smooth on my calves, comforting for a second. But then I pushed harder than the other times I tried, much harder. After a bit I moved my legs higher on the tree, and did it with the two needles at once, thrusting and trying to scrape, till it hurt too much and I stopped. There was a hollow in the loam where my head pressed from arching, but I couldn't break him away from me. Only blood would come. . . . So I had to marry Tom Thwaite. But it changed nothing. Nor what my mother said did, about marriage being good for me, and Tom being a fine strong lad. She lied on both counts. She went on about plenty of other girls in the village in the family way having to get married, I wasn't the only one, it was the accepted thing. There was no point arguing

*with her. Not once she was on her high horse, there wasn't.
I didn't want what was his inside me. Never. I didn't
want him. I told him no, over and over, as he pulled me
down on the grass, shushing me and pinning me. That's
all it took to give it me, put hell inside me, one time, and
it was done in a lousy second what I could never change,
once he'd made me still by slapping me hard across my
mouth, a second, that's all; before he'd finished whim-
pering, the damage was in me. I looked at the blood soaked
into the paper under the needles, and repeated, It has to
be Tom Thwaite in me, it has to be, it can't be anyone
else, it can't. All those times against the bathroom floor,
the towel, when my father. There, I've said it. Father,
father, yes, my own father, my dad, him bastard him, my
f — . . . The razor: in his hand menacing, telling me to
take them off if he wanted to watch and not drag the
knickers down himself; pushed against my neck warning
what would happen if I told anyone what he did; under
my pillow to remind me, if he was on nights, he wasn't
that far away. My father . . . Why hadn't his seed ever
started to grow in me, I couldn't stop thinking. His, or
his from Riddon Moor, it would have come to the same
in the end. Once it was in you, what you'd struggled NO
to, leeching for a life you didn't have to give, what did it
matter what color eyes or hair it would have. Worse was,
you had to be part of it, and it, them, had to be part of
you, both mean bastards. Whatever you hear I didn't go
after Tom Thwaite. I never did. I wanted none of this.
Marriage. That's what they called it. For Christ's sake.
Never. He wanted no different from what my soddin' father
did, and nothing else. Took it the same way. Rough. When*

he wasn't after that, a bit of Jack and Jill as he called it, it were dominoes and beer. No time for his kids as I ever saw. He was never home. Wanted them no more than what I did. But he was cock proud. . . . When I looked at them I couldn't help seeing him. They were his not mine. They were him. One time when I'd had enough I moved out. Took a room in Longton. Left Hazel in a playpen where I knew he'd find her when he came for his tea before he went down the pub. He found her all right, took her straight round my mother's, dumped her there. She came after me at work, said I had to take her back 'cause she was afraid what her Linden might do to the little girl. It was "her Linden" all of a sudden. I grabbed the railings by the factory gate and shook, then turned and let her have one across the face. All the time she'd known about what he did to me. Under the same roof yet she never said a thing, never bloody lifted a hand against him even when her own eye was blacked and I begged her help me put an end to it. I shouldn't have hit her. She'd done what she could in other ways. It was a week or more before I went back to collect his kid and take her home. I wanted so bad again to leave soon as I walked through the door. I nearly did, but I feared what my mother said because I knew if I left my father would get his dirty . . . I could never let that happen to her if I could help it. So I stayed, figuring when I had enough money I'd leave again, take the kids with me. If anything worked out that did because before the young one was a year old Tom Thwaite was gone and I never saw him again. I had a job and somewhere to live so I stopped thinking about going, just got on with it. It would've been no easier anyplace else 'cause what I was running from would be running with me. I'd learned that much. I did my duty, I suppose, though some would say different, tried to help them but it wasn't with any love. I couldn't find a way to that. Soppy, you'll think it sounds, I know, but it's not meant to. . . . Sometimes I felt like a pig eating her own litter. . . . In the end, not so long before he left us, I got so I didn't know who was doing it to me half the time 'cause Tom Thwaite smelled like him, smelled like my father. But if it were Tom Thwaite from the pub or him from the grave come for me in bed, when I knew he was going to beat me or have me or both, I got to lying on my back, open-legged, as if I was willing, and I'd watch the amber from the lamp in the road come soft through the lace, playing gentle across the ceiling, waiting, ready to steer him in my bum, always enough drink in him not to notice the difference, so I could see myself shit on him as he shoved after what they'd always robbed me of.

Before the sunlight comes through the crack between the curtains onto my face to wake me I'm dreaming. On a tufted bog, at sunset, there seem to be three of me. Two of them are more me than the third. One of the more me's is climbing a ladder. The ladder is made of dust but the dust holds me up. The hands on the rungs have bloody stubs, no fingers. I'm already high in the air. I am climbing slowly, never taking my eyes off the other easily recognizable me below for more than a second. The me I'm watching is cutting down the length of a felled tree with a mortise and tenon saw. The tree is so long it disappears into the distance in both directions.

As I'm being watched by the sawing me I (the third me) press my throat. I feel it in the same place as I saw, but not as I climb. Next I prod my belly. The same happens. The sawing me feels it in the same place as the third me; the climbing me feels nothing. The third me begins to brighten, begins to look much more like the other two of me. As the brightness increases I can see the third me has women's parts. The me on the ladder can't look at myself. The ladder crumbles to a pile. That me is gone. The third me stands laughing on the pile of dust the ladder made. The sawing me looks at myself inside my trousers. My parts are male. I look along the tree. A few feet away a knife and fork, operating under their own power, deliver food from a plate to an invisible mouth, which takes all they give it, then asks for money. The third me starts kissing myself, beckoning me with both arms outstretched to come to me. I can't let go of the saw. The third me is gone. A red daisy grows from the dust. A woman in a broad-rimmed hat, a veil over her face, walks by. She kisses the flower. It changes color. She picks up the knife, fork, plate, throws them at me. A cock crows. She strides out to where the bog is muddy. The late rays of the sun dance on her hat. She sinks quickly. . . . I turn away from the light then open my eyes.

Don't know what time I got back to my room last night. I didn't leave the old quarry till late. Clouds had turned the water almost black by then. Remember as I passed the garbage tip there was nothing in the night light to distinguish it from a mound of earth that occurred there naturally; the only sign was a trace of rotting in the otherwise balmy air. Engines were moving in the goods yard. I took the path to the viaduct instead. I shouldn't have.

Tried to concentrate on walking, where I was treading, because the path was bumpy. I didn't want to mash the leg up any worse with a fall. But like I'm doing now I kept drifting back to what she said. Couldn't keep my mind on walking. She said it more than once, I'd let her down when I left, that she expected me to come back, that when she found out from some poacher I'd carved her name in the table in my hut she thought I would, soon, because doing that meant I cared about her. It made no difference that we were young then. That was no excuse for her. She kept it all alive, me alive, with the hope I'd turn up. She said I must have too, else why did I go back after all that time when it was too late. Too late for her maybe. There was more anger than forgiving when she said I was a fool to go back expecting to find her willing, untouched by the years between. . . . I was a fool for dreaming it'd be the same. . . . But she'd hear none of it when I tried to tell her what she'd done was no different from what she said I had. Didn't call her a fool. She said she'd let go of it in the end, which is more than I'd done. Then again she also said she caught hold of a thought once in a while of what might have been. She had it fixed in her head I'd betrayed her. She never let go of that.

I was brooding over her, her thinking about what might have been, as I got to the viaduct. What bloody good was what might have been. She put me on the bus with a bellyful of what might have been, and what couldn't be because she wouldn't let it; never even waved, just turned to go back to her kitchen, miserable, to be on her own, miserable again. There was no what might have been. Why did she try to hold on to a bit of nothing. I asked why, like you do when you know there's no answer, when you know it's no sodding use, most to make yourself feel less of a fool, as you try to force sense where it don't go. Load of old crap is what might have been.

I punched the metal with my fist. Then hit it with the other one. Then went at it both fists punching. It was the metal I hit the first few times. Then it was her husband I was pounding until I dropped him with one that broke his nose then started on Linden Sapper, who was standing black behind him with his pit helmet on, even harder punching until there was no wind left in him, until I broke his ribs so his rotten lungs couldn't get any more and he fell, on top of Tom Thwaite, his tongue hanging out covered in blood and dust, till I kicked his safety lamp in, then there was glass on it too, and I punched once more and it was her I hit as the train thundered over the viaduct.

I staggered off in knots, trying to convice myself it has to come down to something solid in the end, not this. Clay or coal, steel or wood. How you do with one of them. Whether you paint a plate or fire it, turn a screw or make a table. Whether you get paid for what you do while you're here is what counts. Who gives a fuck about the other stuff, what gets you all tangled up inside. Who, eh? No bugger and that's the flaming truth. Clay or coal, steel or wood. What's solid lasts and what lasts is worth something, but not this. What it boils down to, long after you're done for, is solid. You aren't part of that so as you ever know.

I was still unraveling as I came off the path into Edges Road. By then wanting no more to do with her, not giving a damn what happened to her. But I couldn't stop seeing her roll in the dirt and rub it into herself the day she knew for real what he'd done to her meant. I hadn't gone more than a few yards down Edges Road when Freddie Snape (he drinks in the Flea) rolls out of the entry and steadies himself on the lamppost. He put out an arm as I reached him and blocked the way.

"Her's locked me out, the bitch," he said.

"Oh yeah," I said.

"Wife's barred the bastard door."

He swayed and had to take his arm down, needing both of them to get himself stable again.

"Her's done it before," he said. "Thinks I'm pissed. I'm not pissing pissed, I's telling yer. Not spissed, never."

"Yeah?"

"Fuckin' right yeah, who's pissed. You pissed, are yer. Don't call me pissed. Watch this then. Touch my cock with both hands and skip."

He did neither. Just managed to get his hands back to the post before he keeled over.

"Skip and a jump. Man can't have a piddling pint without all his frigging missus kicking him out. What's it comin' to, eh. . . . Be laying us steelworkers off next. . . . I know . . . You ain't tellin' me they . . . Locked me fucking out, she did, the swine. . . . Reckon I know you from somewhere."

"Yeah?"

"Yeah. I sccn you before."

"Yeah?"

"Yeah."

"Don't think so, mate."

"You play darts for the Dog."

"Not me, mate."

"You bloody sure?"

"Ought to know if I do, didn't I."

"You takin' the piss or what?"

"All I said was I don't play for the Dog."

There was no point asking him if he knew the late racing results.

"Where've I seen you then?" he said. "Top of no big slag heap, I ain't that drunk, you know."

"Not sure as you have."

"Women. Shit. You don't have no woman, do yer. Best off without. You're lucky you's not got one to lock you out. Leave 'em alone, I'm telling you."

"Listen, I'm off. G'night."

"Tryin' be funny. What's that leg done?"

"Mind how you go."

"Here, I don't like the look of you. . . . Had bigger than you for breakfast. Think you can beat me, d'you. . . . I'll piss all over you, knock the fucking stuffin' out. No bugger messes round with Freddie Snape and gets . . . C'mon, yer fucker."

He stuck his fists up. Sort of.

"Not with me, pal . . . No bugger, I'm telling yer. . . . So you don't have a woman, ain't it a pity . . . Nothin' do with me, all right . . . You fucker, I'll show yer."

"Please yourself."

He pushed me.

"I'm fucking telling yer, sunshine. No fucking buttercups here, pal. Ain't my fault yer missus left you for
another fella, understand. . . . Never mess with another
man's woman . . . Lay us off, they will . . . What's up
with you, I'll fucking show you."

He took a swing at me. Missed by a mile.

"Listen, mister, go tell it the fairies," I said.

"Don't call me no fairy . . . If she won't take yer back
tough shit, I say. . . . You fuck fairies, I'll show you."

He swung again. Got nearer this time. I pushed him
out of the way and moved on. When he got back to the
lamppost he cursed his wife and me to the end of the
road. Ended up shouting I was having it off with his
missus.

But that was last night making out I didn't know Freddie Snape, saying I didn't want any more to do with her,
rattling on so. That was last night. I look at my hands.
They're a mess. Sore. Swollen. It's another day. Sun's
shining again. What got into me. Those tablets or what.
Got a little crazy. The leg feels fine. I lift the blankets.
No more blood's come through. All my toes working.
No fishing today. Won't be time with all I've got to sort
out. Insurance form to collect from the broker and fill
out. That'll be a bastard. Sticky questions. Looking for a
loophole not to pay you. Small-print merchants. Had to
let it out somehow. If I ever bump into Tom Thwaite . . .
What was I supposed to do. So I went a little . . . It's
what I want . . . Yes, her. Still. Nearly started on Freddie

Snape. Pissed as a rat. Would've been wrong in his condition to lay one on him. He was asking for it. I'll need the police report. Down to the cop station for that and a million bloody questions. You said you were doing forty miles an hour. About forty miles an hour, sorry sir, and you signaled to turn into Murphy's Lane but you didn't see the car. We know it was a car hit you, sir, or you hit the car. Fresh skid marks and a bit of bumper what broke off. You were doing forty miles an hour, you say, down Parson's Road and you saw a cat and slowed down for the turn but you never saw the car after you signaled. About midnight it was, you say. Forty miles an hour. A cat. A pillar box. But you never saw a car. You don't remember getting hit. I remember seeing Hazel. Breaking the speed limit, weren't we, sir. I remember seeing Hazel. What happened to her must have happened to hundreds of kids. But she could . . . Doesn't make it right, I'm not saying that, for Christ's sake. . . . She maybe could try to let bygones be . . . These fingers look broken. . . . No use her staying like that. It's done and gone. He's dead. What good's it going to do her. Even if she doesn't want me, what good. That dream. Was it her in the mud sinking? Was it anything to do with me and Billy Filmer? Have to call at the SS office about the sick pay. I'm all paid up with the stamps. So you hit the car speeding, sir. I hit no car. Car hit me. I never saw no car. Came from nowhere. . . . Got to get out of bed. Get a paper.

I have a bit of trouble getting dressed because of my hands. I sit on the bed and roll up a fag. That's not easy either. I make a pig's arse of it. But it tastes good. I finish it and roll a better one and light it up. I can't find my stick. Must have left it at the viaduct. Hospital said they wanted it back. I put on my jacket and check the betting slip's there. I set off for the paper shop to get the racing results. I'm doing all right without the stick. If Irish Display's won I'll go back with the money to see Hazel Saturday. She said what she liked best was doing her little garden. I'll take her some bedding plants. Might change her mind. Be nothing more to lose if she don't.